It's Murder: On Hat Island

A Gedney Island Mystery Featuring Lily Martian

By

N. R. De Witte

First published by AuthorHouse 06/11/04

ISBN: 1-4184-6282-9 (e-book)
ISBN: 1-4184-4751-X (Paperback)

This book is printed on acid free paper.

Dedicated in loving memory of

Mikey.

iii

Special thanks to:

R.A.M. because you said I could do it,

Dave for giving me endless pushes,

Mary for her kindness and encouragement,

Friends who endlessly endured me reading to them,

and to David Dilgard and Margaret Riddle of the Everett Public Library who helped dig up the sparse information available about Gedney Island.

Prologue

November 22, 1875

The chill of November winds hit their bare arms and shins with such force that at first they were tempted to turn back toward the mainland. But hateful determination spurred them on. They had a mission to accomplish. Rowing quietly through the salt brine, the sloop's oars dripping silent rings of colorful phosphorescence sparkles into the water, they edged close to the shore. Stepping out into the ankle-deep frigid salt water they noiselessly pulled the 14-foot sloop up onto the beach, far enough so that an incoming tide could not take their escape vessel away in the darkness. The night was black, except for the glow of the yonder cabin window, and stars twinkling in the sky with the occasional light of the moon as it passed behind hazing clouds.

The steady lap of the bay upon the sandy shore and gusts of sporadic wind were the only night sounds. Stealthily they crept over the shells and drift that littered the sandy beach. Quietly, they climbed over the logs that made a natural bulkhead, thus protecting the vegetation of the island inland. They could hear sounds now, the soft lowing of the cattle he kept on the island and the occasional chirp of fowl. And, what they had so guarded against, the discovering bark of a dog.

Cautiously they stopped and hid behind a large clump of brush hedged within alder trees, until the dog quieted. Minutes seemed like hours as they patiently waited until they deemed it safe enough to venture toward the rustic, hand-hewn cabin. Now in the moon's beam, they could just make out the acrid smelling wood smoke, combined with the aromatic blend of bacon, billowing from the chimney. Upon closer inspection, they could see the parade of a shadow against one of the oilskin cabin windows. He was there, the bastard, in his self-imposed exile. No doubt counting his wealth, or drinking his fill of whiskey. While others on the mainland scraped by each day to get a decent meal, he luxuriated on the island, tending his livestock and harvesting his apple crop, which he sold to mainlanders for outrageous prices. At desperate times when food sources were low he had money jingling in his pockets and after his wares were sold, would carouse through town, drinking, gaming and lustily carrying on with the town's women; welcomed or not. All the while boasting of his good fortune and reported hoard of gold stashed away on his island home.

He would boast no more. Tonight was the end. Drink heartily, "Stuhey," for it will be your last drink. With those thoughts, both men withdrew their muskets from their back slings, checked gunpowder and approached the cabin, now unconcerned of any noise they made.

Chapter One

November 22, 1995

I couldn't scream. I tried, but no sound would come out of my mouth. I lie there in mute terror, eyes tightly shut, pulse racing and trying to force sound from a larynx paralyzed by fear. It was with great relief that I discovered I was awake. I was hot. Sweat beaded between my breasts, and my worn cotton gown clung to my thighs.

Furious howling and incessant banging gnawed at me. Groggily and somewhat disoriented I tried to determine the source of noise. Ah yes, the much predicted windstorm.

Evidently the weather forecasters were correct for once, judging from the sounds of nature bellowing its gall around me. I rolled to my side to catch a glance at the night stand clock, but I could see nothing but blackness. Other than the shadowed moon glow filtering through my bedroom sheers, the night was dark and so was my cabin.

Waking up from a bad dream was unnerving. Storms around the Northwest were a dime a dozen, but it wasn't so with dreams, at least in my case and especially those of nightmare quality. I usually slept soundly - almost the sleep of the dead. I shuddered, perhaps it served me right, listening to the droll, monotonous voice of the medical transcription tape earlier in the evening. It would have given anybody nightmares, even the most stoic. But the volume of work I had to complete for Dr. Ivers couldn't wait for a decent hour; "sick folks don't wait," he always said.

Scrunching up the pillows and smoothing the blankets, I noticed that the banging sound had increased along with the howling of the wind.

I was vexed with myself when I decided the noise was coming from the front screen-door I had neglected to lock earlier in the evening. The island harbormaster, Matt Andrews, had cautioned me mid-day to prepare for the storm. "Get those candles out, Lily, and make sure to batten down the hatches!" He had warned. I do not heed good advice. Cuddled under my comforter, I thought about staying in bed and putting up with the racket, or making the supreme effort and feeling my way through my small home to latch the door and thus incur peace. I elected the first. After all, a little noise wouldn't hurt me and I would much rather put up with racket than injure myself trying to latch my door. Light of foot I am not and any kind of obstacle in my path most often results in some calamity, mostly to my person. Let the clatter lull me back to sleep, as it certainly did not seem to wake my dog, Chuck. He slept soundly at the foot of my bed, literally.

Trying to shift my foot from under Chuck was no easy task. I yanked and was rewarded with a number of sensational pinpricks of pain. My foot had apparently fallen asleep from Chuck's weight. Well, at least some part of my body had had some rest tonight. Finally gaining a comfortable and cozy position, screen-door still banging, I bravely recalled my dream with a shudder:

Our chief physician at the medical clinic I work for, Dr. Ivers, was racing toward me with outstretched arms. Definitely not for the purpose of a hug, as one hand clutched a hideous instrument capable of inflicting grave bodily injury. I couldn't recall the exact tool of torture, but didn't doubt that my subconscious had selected a facsimile of the odious scalpel that Dr. Ivers had detailed on the transcription tape. I remembered clearly his dictation of the future excision of a patient's ganglion cyst and could picture him as he hunched over his cluttered desk studying patient charts and chicken-scratched medical jargon while speaking into his recorder; however, during the course of his recitation, my dream state changed his appearance. His thin, sparse gray hair became thick and full with unruly streaks of gray. His eyes, usually bright blue and twinkling, changed to almost a black-brown. Steely in appearance, they stared hard and unyielding at something or someone with absolute hatred. The face was hard to discern as it wavered and I could not get a clear picture. It seemed, however, to take on a bearded and weathered look, yet in the next instant wavered again into a ghoulish mass of blood and membrane. Dr. Ivers had become morphic, for I had just dreamed of a man I had never seen before in my life, and one that for good reason sent chills up my spine and frightened me to bits.

I didn't want to dwell on the dream any longer, as it was quite unsettling to me. I didn't understand it, nor did I want to analyze it. I snuggled deeper under the covers and willed myself to be content to hear the screen-door banging, Chuck snoring, and relieved that at least the trees surrounding the cabin were out of reach should the force of nature cause them to fall.

Morning peeked through my bedroom window sheers with a blaze of November sun. I had slept fairly well considering my nightmare and the racket of the wind, both of which didn't seem so bad now. I was, however, cold. Glancing once again at the night stand to see if the power returned during the night, I noted that nothing illuminated on the clock's dial. Morning's daylight at least let me enjoy the picture of my twin sons, Garrett and Garth, smiling from inside the oak frame perched next to the clock. I missed them with an intensity that made my insides ache. Nineteen years old, they lived in Oregon, attending Portland State University, their father's, my ex-husband's, Alma Mater. They would have relished last night's storm with the zest of youth, clamoring for downed wood for the stove and scouting about for any apparent storm damage to report. They had been great fun for me in their adolescent years; company during an extremely lonely marriage and healing balm for the soreness of divorce.

I reminisced for a few more minutes, rolling over onto my back and fortifying myself with mental exercises of getting ready for the day without the benefit of a hot shower, and most importantly, coffee.

After a few minutes of self-pity, I gingerly make my way from the bed into the small adjoining bath. Hurriedly, I tried to freshen-up, splashing ice-cold water into my face, thereby becoming fully awake, and colder still. Startled green eyes, my best feature other than my girlish charm, stared back at me from the bathroom mirror. My cheeks were rosy from the burst of cold water and my short blond hair stood out at unattractive angles about my head. Best to wear a hat, I decided. Other than slapping some lipstick on (okay, so I'm somewhat vain), I rapidly dressed for warmth in Levi's, heavy socks and a thick sweatshirt which proclaimed, "Scandinavian, and Proud of It!"

After sprucing up, I went into my small living area where I crossed to the wood stove. It was the main heat source of my cabin, other than the hopelessly inadequate wall heaters, presently defunct because of the power outage. Opening the door to the stove, I was thankful that a few embers still glowed amidst the ash. Feeding the tiny coals with bits of kindling and rolled newspaper I had stashed beside the stove in a basket, within minutes I was able to warm my hands at the fire as well as heat some water for instant coffee. Just the realization of the fact of coffee was enough to help brighten the day. I still didn't know the time. With my luck and the way my eyes felt, raw and strained, it was probably only 6:00 in the morning; I should have slept in longer.

Having enjoyed my first cup of coffee, hot and full of caffeine, though not my usual gourmet brand, I was fortified with enough ambition to continue with my daily exercise routine - hiking the small perimeter of the island on which I live. Officially christened Gedney Island by the Charles Wilkes Expedition in 1841 in honor of New York inventor Jonathon H. Gedney, most locals fondly know it as "Hat." As a young girl I had asked my dad the origin of the name. His reply had been that when boaters cruised by the island, the southwest wind would blow off their hats; thus, "Hat" Island. Only as an adult did I discover a more plausible reason - that the island was formed in a shape of a hat. Though in my humble opinion, it resembles a misshapen beret at best.

Hat Island, one of the Puget Sound's many islands, is located in the western region of Washington State. Situated in the midst of Port Gardner Bay on Possession Sound, it offers views of the Olympic and Cascade Mountains, and Alki Point. Native Americans once used the island as a stopover while on fishing expeditions and the island also harbored bootleggers during Prohibition. "Hat" is about two miles in length and one half mile in width, so a walk around the entire perimeter, tides cooperating, is not an impossible feat and can take the average walker about two hours from start to finish. I did not know that today was to be a much different hike than usual, one I was not likely to forget for several years to come.

N. R. De Witte

Chapter Two

With my hike in mind, I peered out the front room window and saw that the weather was still unsettling. White caps pitched against the green sea, frothing and lathering as if in dance. The brightness of the day did not alleviate the fact that the wind was still gusting, though not as fiercely as in the night. The temperature was chilly in my home, but out of doors looked even more so. My walk was going to be brisk, that was for certain, so I searched for a pair of gloves in anticipation of the bone-chilling air, shrugged into my fleece-lined denim jacket, called for Chuck and headed out the door.

My spaniel emerged from the back bedroom and trotted up the pine floors with a clicking of toenails. He had remained snuggled in my bed, emanating his salty sea stench in the bedding, and of course not budging when I had earlier gotten up to get ready (almost as if he knew that he needed the extra rest for his daily exercise routine with his master.) This time of year and with Chuck such a classic water dog, it was hard to keep him hygienic. Just as difficult, or perhaps even more so, was the chore of not allowing him in the cabin, let alone on my bed.

We raced up the graveled drive, or rather Chuck did. In my late thirties, I don't race anywhere any more. I paused a moment to scan the area of my home - to make sure it did not have any storm damage. Only a few fallen branches littered the grounds, and my Jeep Wrangler, which was parked in the drive. My simple cabin stood invitingly charming, eaves covered in moss, with weathered wood siding and trim of forest green. Wisps of smoke curled up from the chimney and I could see the healthy supply of chopped alder, which lay neatly stacked against the old unused, out-house to the rear of the cabin. My sons had begrudgingly chopped and stacked throughout a month's stay during summer break to make sure mom would be plenty warm for the winter. Both pleased and relieved that I had no apparent damage to worry about, I turned and followed Chuck down the drive and up to the island's main road.

I habitually begin and end my walks at the island's minuscule marina, which is just about an eighth of a mile from my cabin. The marina is situated behind a breakwater on the northeast side of the island; (the tiny cove is accessible only to and for the use of island residents, property owners, or invited guests). This morning, however, I chose to cut diagonally across the island to survey the storm damage from on top as well as from the beach.

Passing the quaint duck pond, which lies adjacent to the island's tennis court, I was surprised to see the ducks, both elegant mallard and dull-brown hen, scooting along the pond. Apparently they had not gotten blown away, nor were they hovering in fright, snuggled in their floating duck house in the middle of the large pond terrorized by last night's storm. Chuck seemed pleased to see them as well, pacing the side of the pond and whining - I could tell he was contemplating a swim to see if he could catch the game. With a firm, "come along," he reluctantly turned and followed me east down the road.

I surveyed the wind damage as I walked. On several sections of the road, alder branches were splayed as well as that of fir. But that was about the only damage I could see; however homes were located sporadically within the folds of alder and fir, and there could be damage that I had not noticed. Guilt hit me for a moment as I should have checked up on my neighbors, Sanford and Vivian Wardell, who lived two lots to the north of me.

The Wardell's were an elderly couple who had been on the island less than two years. They were from

California, ill prepared for the harshness of northwest storms. Sanford reminded me of a physical replica of Roy Rogers, complete with smiling dimples. But as Roy Rogers' smile lit up his eyes, Sanford's remained dull and cold as a lizard's, thus the end of the similarity. In tandem, Vivian was a spitting image of Dale Evans. Complete with the bouffant hair-do, but she, as with Sanford, sadly missed Dale's warmth and personality.

Perhaps I was just sore. Ever since the previous August when Chuck had been ill mannered and had helped to weed Vivian's prize petunia patch, things hadn't been exactly cozy between us. I could still envision Sanford's red face and shouting obscenities, as Vivian stood by his side simpering, with clumps of wilted prize petunias clutched in her hands. What a big to-do over flowers, for goodness sake! You would have thought Chuck had crapped on their lounge chairs or helped himself to a steak dinner off their barbecue grill. In retrospect, I acknowledged that because of Sanford and Vivian's age what seemed of less importance to me was of utmost importance to them. But, I also acknowledged that they were as stuck up and pompous as any couple I had met. I frequently wondered why they lived such a remote life at Hat Island when they could be luxuriating in some prime golf course community at Sahalee or Bear Creek in Woodinville, now one of the *in places* in western Washington. My conscious was feeling better about not checking on the Wardell's, and I put them out of my mind as I continued my walk. I was making good time and reached the steep gravel route leading to the beach in less than 20 minutes.

Descending the road, I looked straight out to the bay. White caps were still in disarray. I was not privy to the wildness of the sea the night before and could only imagine the fierceness. Boaters are at the mercy of the sea and the sea is not to be trusted, but to be wary of and respected at all times. Looking out over the water, I was glad not to be venturing across the bay to the mainland today.

Clamoring over the rock bulkhead to the sand below, I headed east on the beach. Chuck, sensing our course, trotted confidently ahead of me. My favorite walk is in this section of the island, past the old gravel bunker established in 1870 by the Hat Island Sand and Gravel Company. It is located on the West Side of the island and about a mile walk from my cabin. Pausing, I stopped and peered at the remnants of the bunker. Much of the gravel on this West Side of the island had been used during World War I for a local merchant's road construction business. It was thought that island clay, because of its high silicone content, would be of value in commercial use, but that never materialized. So through the years the bunker, once a valued storage unit, had slowly deteriorated. Cement eroded with each splash of saltwater, causing gaping holes on all four sides of its original box-like structure. The accompanying wharf for gravel-laden barges formerly constructed of heavy planking and once huge and towering was now incongruent nubs, barely breaking the surface of the incoming tide. All trace of the once noble

17

structure was gone, no doubt wasting away below the sea at the bottom of the bay reef. Time goes by so slowly, yet so quickly. I could remember the wharf vividly, yet now it seemed it had never existed.

Just past the bunker lies Section H of the island. The island is cordoned off in sections; to distinguish not only residential areas but also available land parcels as well. Section H has roughly 30 homes, some of which are downright posh. So far removed from the cabin of my childhood (as well as my present abode), they stand tall and proud and in my mind, out of place. Tile roofing, clapboard siding, rock fireplaces and innumerable windows to encompass all possible view, dwellings here could vie against any fancy mainland home. And though the island was only accessible by boats, full time residents occupied a few of the homes. Retirement made it possible, and the convenient island location made it probable, since there were no tides to deal with. The island ferry, "The Holiday" conveniently operated on weekends and one day mid-week, so needs could be met.

Living here was akin to being away from it all, yet within 20 minutes of "civilization." Yes, the island was a perfect place to live, and that is why I lived here, though in less extravagant quarters.

Chuck was quite a ways ahead of me. Ever watchful of my pet, I was a bit concerned when he disappeared behind some rocks near the bulkhead. Sure enough, eventually he emerged and started to run past me, some malodorous object clamped in his jaws. Most likely fish bones or rotten crab bait. I needed to pry the matter from his mouth, before he swallowed it and choked on the bones. The beach can wreak havoc on pets that find turkey, fish and chicken bones washed up on shore - the result of crabbing and fishing expeditions.

Having saved my pet from choking, or at the least indigestion, I continued up the beach. The tide was out and the smell of salt emanating from the exposed tide flats was strong, yet appealing. Gulls circled overhead, searching for meals that the bay may have uncovered for them. I watched them for a moment before peering at the host of houses I was walking past. Though most of the homes looked empty, I noticed that two had smoke wafting from their chimneys. As I passed one home, I saw the owner standing by the window, coffee cup in hand. Raising my hand in greeting, I motioned to my wrist, hoping that he would catch my play of the need for the time. No dice, he just waved in recognition. Well, I reflected, can't be too early, Dan Compton was up and about. He drank from his cup in casual relaxation, his white hair and beard illuminated in the early morning light through the large expanse of picture window.

Chuck had managed to retrieve his pride and once again was quite a bit ahead of me. My body temperature was warming up because of the exercise and I was enjoying the scenery: The incoming tide sliding onto the outstretch of beach, and more cries of the gulls as they apparently reveled in their discovery of abundant food sources. At times like this, I felt so at peace, almost happy. In reality I hadn't been happy in years - content, perhaps, but not happy.

True happiness encompasses all facets of life: peace, companionship, and love. I had two of the three. That wasn't enough. I longed for the storybook romance, the happily ever after part. Even after a decade long miserable marriage, I still hoped and yearned for something truly wonderful. I thought I had reached that pinnacle of bliss two years after my divorce when I had met a man and fell madly, passionately in love. Plans of living a life full of love and sharing was planned, all to end a few months later without even a simple explanation or goodbye. Sunk into a deep depression for several months, I blamed God and everything I could for my loss. Eventually I was able to snap out of it and, ludicrous it may seem at times, part of me (just a bit, mind you,) still clung to the belief that somewhere, someday I would find my prince charming again, my "soul mate." I could then pass this life experiencing all it had to offer. A perfect home, adoring children, and the true and constant love of a mate. With a wry smile, I remembered my mother telling me when I was younger and poring over romance novels, "life isn't like that. There is no such thing as what is in those books." Perhaps, Mom, you were right. How I wished to prove you wrong.

Before I could feel more sorry for myself, Chuck's harsh barking interrupted me. I was concerned, as Chuck was a very mild animal - never given over to hysterical barking such as now - something was wrong, seriously wrong.

Chapter Three

Chuck's barking was reaching a fevered pitch. I could only imagine the worst, as I dashed toward the sound. It was hard to be speedy. This part of the beach was the rockiest on the island. Rocks in average circumference of five to six inches littered the area. It was faster to leap from one large stone to another than to try and pick my way between them. Finally, I was able to locate Chuck's whereabouts, behind a very large uprooted tree. Now a magnificent piece of drift, it resembled a hand unfolding and beckoning toward the heavens. *What an understatement.*

Rounding to the back of the drift, I spied my spaniel, standing legs askance, neck hair raised, now yipping almost forlornly at something just a few feet away from him. I was concerned at first that it may be sea otters known to nest in the nearby rock bulkhead. I would have been pleased had it been, for I was shocked - no, much more than that, horrified - to see a body on the sand. A human body and a certainly dead body. I stepped back and gasped.

·   Pulling Chuck away from the scene, I yanked him toward the bay and fresh air. As gulls cried above me, I cried below pulling my pet over the stones and through the soft sand to the water's edge. I sank to my knees, the moistness seeping into my Levi's, cuffs of my jacket, and gloves, though I really didn't notice at first. All I could think of was that after a lifetime of living on the island, I had always subconsciously worried about discovering something dreadful on the beach, other than the infrequent dead cow (awash from Whidbey), dog or seal. I often cringed when the local news would broadcast that someone was missing from a fishing expedition or leisure activity on the water. I never wanted to witness such a find on my island. Now I had.

I gagged repeatedly on the beach, and it took a while for me to get my composure intact. Finally, keeping a firm grasp of Chuck's collar, I edged back to the area of the body. I had to pull Chuck along with me, for he seemed much more reluctant than I did. Who could blame him? It was not that I had a morbid curiosity, but an underlying thought that perhaps I could help the poor victim in some way. At a distance, I could see that my intentions would prove fruitless. The victim was lying prone, arms akimbo. I couldn't tell whether it was male or female, but decided by size and clothing that it was most likely male. Mercifully, the person was clothed, though sodden and torn. One shoe was missing. The head was turned at an odd angle. Good, I thought to myself, I don't want to see the face. Peering more closely, I noticed that the short, plastered, silver-gray hair did not adequately cover a gouge in the cranium that sent my insides in a riot once again. Even the seaweed interspersed over the wound could not hide the damage this unfortunate man had incurred. He had a hole in his head the size of a damn baseball - and most of the stuffing had definitely oozed out. Stomach churning, determined that I had seen enough to know that this was the real McCoy, I turned and ran back toward Section H faster than I had run since junior high.

What happened in the course of the next three hours, I can't totally recall; shock, I guess. Everything was blurry. Dan Compton had answered my hysterical rapping almost immediately. His smile at thinking I had stopped by for morning coffee and idle chit-chat slowly drained from his face as took in my disheveled appearance: hat askew, sodden jeans, and white face. As I stammered my discovery, he led me into his house, deposited me on the living room couch and called 911, after which he placed a full high ball glass of brandy firmly into my badly shaking, gloved hands. We both sat stoically, draining our brandy glasses (he had joined me),

waiting for the authorities. I still
did not know the time of day.

The island is under the
jurisdiction of Snohomish County.
Taxes are paid to the county and,
therefore, while phone service is
Island County's domain, everything
else belongs to Snohomish County and
has for well over 100 years.

Dan and I sat silently in front
of his fire, brandy number two
clasped in our hands. I had managed
to pry off my wet and sandy gloves -
the warmth of the brandy had not
only scorched a path down my throat
and into my stomach but flowed into
my fingers as well so at least they
were no longer numb. The sheriff's
department homicide squad had
arrived on the golf green via
helicopter. Matt Andrews met them at
the clubhouse, transporting officers
down the gravel drive in the
island's used school bus, normally
used to pick up and drop off island
ferryboat passengers. They had
stopped at Dan's, before continuing
toward where I had found the body.

It seemed such a short time
before one of the officers returned.

Knocking, he came into Dan's living room and squatted directly in front of me.

"I understand you found the body, Miss," he began slightly hesitating as if to ascertain my condition before he continued on.

"Yes," I replied, looking up from my lap to meet his eyes. "We did, Chuck my dog, and me."

"I see. Did you touch anything, or see anything else out of the ordinary?" At the negative shake of my head, he continued, "How about people, or boats close to the beach?"

I replied softly, "No. I didn't see anything. He's missing a shoe."

Surprise flickered in his hazel eyes. "May I have your name, please? I need to complete your statement." He reached into his overcoat pocket and removed a small spiral notebook and pen. He flipped the page, clicked the pen and began to write.

I gave him my full name, spelling the last one for him. Then gave my island address and phone number. He briefly glanced up at me when I spelled my name (was that a smirk I detected?) - I got that a lot. For whatever reason my family pronounced our last name *Martin*, even though it was spelled Martian. As a kid I was constantly razzed about the whereabouts of my antennas or spaceship. Being wed was the only good thing, besides my sons, that my crummy marriage had given me. Johnson was a good, sound, and error-free last name. But, upon my divorce, wanting to rid myself of anything remotely associated with my former husband; I had resumed using my maiden name of Martian. And, as a result, more spelling difficulties as well as the occasional snicker.

After spelling my last name, I explained the walk, Chuck's barking and finding the body. The officer was very quiet as he made notes. I studied him as he scratched along in his notebook, occasionally frowning as he completed a sentence and began a new one. He was middle-aged, craggy-faced, salt and pepper colored hair, thinning on top. Medium height and weight, solemn faced as if he carried too many stories inside him. He looked a bit puzzled when he asked me where he could reach me during the day should he have questions and I repeated my phone number. I explained that I was self-employed as a medical transcriber, utilizing a home computer to send and receive my work. He noted that information as well, though I wondered at the importance. Vital or not, he seemed intent on getting all the facts.

Satisfied that he would not get any more pertinent data from me, the officer stood up and thanked me for the information as well as for my time.

"If you think of anything else, Miss Martin, please call me." He handed me his business card. After he left, I glanced at the card in my shaking hand. Detective Nick Anton, Snohomish County Sheriff's Office. Maybe he was Italian that would explain his dark looks. Oh who cared - I was beginning to get irrational, a bit tipsy from the brandy and suddenly extremely fatigued.

I did not remember the walk back to my cabin, as I was still in somewhat of a daze. I did know the time, finally, just after 3:00 PM and already beginning to become dark. It seemed to me that the entire day had been dark, after beginning so brightly.

N. R. De Witte

Chapter Four

I discovered upon entering my home that the electricity had come back on while I was gone. Blinking lights greeted me from the microwave, stereo and VCR. I sighed, not in the mood to set the time on my flashing appliances. While I certainly appreciated the convenience of modern day, I missed the coziness of camping with the light of the propane lantern and candles, which ended when electrical cable was run from the mainland along the sea floor. I started to reach for my tea bags, but grabbed a bottle of wine instead. Though I had brandy earlier, the effects had worn off during my hike home in the cold and I just couldn't deal with life right now fully sober. I needed the dulling of the senses that alcohol provided, however unwise.

Glass in hand, I ventured into the bathroom to take a hot shower. My cold 'spit bath' earlier along with finding the body had left me with an intensely dirty feeling - both in mind and body. Undressing, I stepped into the steaming shower and stood under the cascading droplets, hoping to wash away the events of the day. Memories flooded me just then, perhaps because I was in a vulnerable state. Puget Sound Sea baths in my early years growing up on the island sprang to mind. Until 25 years ago, most water was hauled over from the mainland in five-gallon containers, or collected from gutters the result of frequent Northwest rain showers. There was never enough water to adequately bathe and feel completely "clean." When I was young, my dad would go down to the beach with his towel and bar of soap and take a "bay bath." I was never an active participant in this endeavor. As a child, I wasn't too keen on bathing anyway, and certainly not in freezing salt water.

I concluded my shower, thankful once again for the heavenly supply of hot water that the return of the power had provided. I felt better, more relaxed. Slipping into a cotton terry robe, I rubbed a section of steam off the mirror and stared at my pale reflection. My eyes were sad as well as bloodshot. I applied some moisturizer, towel-dried my hair and then went into the kitchen to refresh my dwindling glass of wine. In the front window of the living room, I looked out to see that dusk had descended. Twinkling lights from passing watercraft sparkled on the water, no doubt on route to close by Langley or Clinton harbors on Whidbey Island. Lights from the Tulalip Reservation, Camano Island and north Whidbey Island were also visible, glittering and twinkling like Christmas lights across the water. I wished I could enjoy the sight more, but still saddened by the events of the day, I turned away from the window. I was beginning to feel somewhat light-headed and most likely needed to eat instead of drink.

Chuck's bark at the door alerted me just moments before someone knocked. In response to my, "Who's there," I was pleased to hear Matt Andrews' voice. I opened the door and gestured him inside.

Matt didn't seem to notice my apparel, or lack of, just grumbled, "Well, lotsa action 'round here today. Darn city-folk poking around, asking questions. Ain't our fault some guy got washed up on shore. Not like we planted him there or somethin."

He stood just inside my door, huffing and puffing, not so much because of physical strain, but with frustration due to the many projects facing him because of the storm and the increased activity resulting from the discovery of a dead body. His face was red, whether from the coldness of outside or stress I didn't know, and his gray eyes were bloodshot. Bits of gray hair poked out of his baseball hat and he looked older than his sixty-six years. A slight man, he could ill afford to get exhausted or overwrought because of his declining

36

health, the age-induced onset of diabetes.

Matt loved the island and had been the caretaker for well over 15 years, ever since retiring from the service. On his list of priorities the island's welfare was first and his well being second.

"Do the police know any more?" I asked. "Like, who the dead person is?" I wanted it over with, the body identified and transported to where it belonged. Family members were no doubt in a quandary about their missing loved one.

Matt spoke, interrupting my thoughts about the dead person's grieving family; "Coroner showed up a while ago. Slapped that sucker in a body bag and hauled it off in our bus, yours truly at the wheel. Enough to give me the creeps. Had to go pick him up at the green, too. Damn green's gonna be all beat up 'cause of those copters," he grizzled. "That and the storm damage make the area look like a war zone. It'll keep me busy all month."

Hat Island developers established the tidy track of golf green in 1962 for usage only by the club's homeowners and invited guests. The course contains two par-3s, six par-4s, and a 470-yard par-5. The topography is mostly flat and the green ringed with trees, which definitely explained Matt's disturbance at all the storm damage.

I shuddered at the thought of riding again in the bus, as I had a vision of a body bag bouncing along the floorboards. I shoved the thought from my mind and asked, "Damage to the course?" (I hope he hadn't noticed I had slurred a bit on the last word, kind of sounded like 'horse' instead of course to my ears.)

Apparently I was safe with my slip, as Matt continued in an even more exasperated tone than before, "Yeah, there are piles of wood every hundred yards or so along the fairways. An' them roads have the usual storm collection of maple, alder and fir. Why I took this job, I'll never know."

"You took it because you love the island and your life here," I gently reminded him. "Sure, there will be a lot of work to do to clean things up, and this incident certainly doesn't help things, but you'll work it out - you always do. Lee can help you; after all, it is part of his job too. (I spoke of Lee Treasure one of our newest Island residents. Lee had been recruited by the island bigwigs as the Golf Pro. Highly energetic and attractive, he rubbed Matt the wrong way.) I knew as soon as I said it, with Matt's grimace, that it was a "no no." Quickly I added, "Anyway, other than the golf course and roads, is there any damage to homes or the marina?"

"Enough. Those wild winds along with a 14 foot tide brought in logs, but 'cuz most of the year-rounders' boats are on the inside of the dock, they didn't hurt nothin. Only bit of damage was the main ferry dock bouncing up and down like some dad burn caterpillar. Knocked one of the sections of the ramp loose. Broke a darned electrical conduit. Hafta move all them boats around there to the north dock until an electrician can get out to repair it. I'm no good with wires, though I did patch the dock t'gether for now with chains and plywood. Some of them piling gotta be replaced though, cuz of rot."

Matt dutifully filled me in on the mishaps of the marina and went on to relate that many of the homes had lost shakes and shingles along with TV antennas. "Remember, Lily, when we didn't have TV. Let alone electricity? Now them days were good. Quiet, peaceful…. Before all the so-called improvements to make life easier. Well, in my opinion, it took the good times away . . . " he trailed off with a far off look in his eyes, no doubt reliving the past when indeed things were more pleasant and less hectic, both here on the island and on the mainland.

With a shake of his grizzled head, he seemed to recall the origin of our conversation and continued on, "Oh, yeah, some trees fell in the yards, few on fences and one on a porch. Ya know that fancy cedar cabin on the East Side? Well, damned maple went clean through the roof, landing right smack in the middle of the living room. Good thing they weren't done building - looks like they'll be patching for some time. Other than that, no real damage. Just the usual trees and firewood a plenty."

"Well, that's good," I replied. I had crossed back to the kitchen to refill my wineglass. "I haven't really checked things out around here other than a quick look-see this morning, but everything seems to be fine. The roof is still holding. Though one of these days, I'm afraid I'll be in for it. Another fierce wind like we had last night, and I'll be dipping into the savings and scouring around to find some cheap roofer to replace the roof!" I attempted a light-hearted laugh that caught in my throat and definitely did not reach my eyes.

"Now Lily, try not to think about that body, and for God's sake, lay off the booze. You know what a lightweight you are. Just make things worse. You can get morose on likker. I should know." Matt admonished me, but gently. I knew what he was referring to, the loss of his wife of 40 years. Matt had tried to ease his pain in alcohol and had developed a drinking problem. He had been able to kick the habit with the help of AA and friends and had been on my case ever since - suggesting that perhaps I drank a bit too much. He'd gotten especially bad since last fourth of July's island potluck at the marina when I had imbibed a bit too much, and he had escorted me home. Well, I didn't embarrass anyone but myself and I had definitely paid for it the next day with a lousy headache and nauseous stomach that had lasted throughout the evening. Why wasn't a horrendous hangover ever enough to make one learn? Especially me?

I smiled a lopsided half-smile and replied, "I just wish I hadn't been the one to find him. I can't seem to get the vision out of my mind. And, I can too handle my liquor. I'm just relaxing. If anyone deserves to after today, I do."

Matt patted me on the shoulder, sighed and left, claiming he had to check on the "city folk" still lurking around the island. Especially, he intoned, "any of them newspaper people." Matt was fiercely protective of the island and residents, a feeling I shared whole-heartedly with him. I called after him to get home early, remember to eat and get some sleep. He either didn't hear me or chose to ignore me with male-only selective hearing.

I didn't feel like eating any supper. Though my stomach rumbled a bit around 7:00 PM. I should have knocked off the wine and gone back to my transcription since the power had returned and I needed to catch up from the day before. But foggy minds do not make fast fingers and I knew better than to attempt even the humblest project. Tomorrow was another day and if I worked my fingers to the bones, I'd be able to catch up on the multitude of transcription postponed by the power outage and the discovery of the body.

N. R. De Witte

Chapter Five

I sat sipping Chardonnay and gazing out the front window at the lights beyond, where everything seemed normal and serene. Hard to imagine that less than 24 hours ago great gusts had greeted the sky along with whirling winds and churning waves. Homes were at the mercy of nature and animals burrowed for cover. Death had occurred on my island. So much for blocking out morbid thoughts, so I took another swallow.

Chuck whimpered and growled at the door. I really wasn't too surprised by the eventual knock. For such a quiet place, the island certainly was teeming with activity today, understandably of course. It seemed that my front door had its share as well.

As I had earlier, I called through the door to ask who was there. A mumbled reply of "police" answered my query. I immediately unlocked the door and swung it wide (not meaning to, but my dexterity was beginning to leave me.)

I noticed upon opening the door that the wind had kicked back up, for Detective Anton stood on the other side of the threshold, his hair standing on end. He was impatiently patting it into place and eyeing Chuck at his feet. Catching my eye, he dropped his hand and extended it toward me. Warmth seemed to emanate from his hazel eyes (could it be my apparel?) "Miss Martian," he ventured (though he pronounced it once again 'Marshun.' Might I have just a moment of your time?"

"Yes, of course. Please come in," I replied. "By the way," I added with what I hoped was emphasis, "My last name is pronounced, Martin, as I told you earlier today." "Remember, no antennas." I said this while stepping aside and almost tripping over the corner of my robe. Sauntering in and looking about, Detective Anton seemed to have an amused smile on his face, as if he knew exactly the correct pronunciation of my name, but savored my response of his error. He was still smiling slightly as he removed his spiral notebook from his overcoat pocket and flipped it open. Removing a pen clipped to his shirt pocket, he poised to write. "Now, Miss Martian, you said that you saw nothing unusual around the beach this morning. No one about, any boats, noise, anything."

"That's right, just Chuck and me. Why, detective?" I asked, "Wasn't this just an unfortunate boating accident? I'm sure by now that someone must have reported something amiss, to the Coast Guard, or something."

"No, nothing from the Coast Guard. In fact, they have discontinued their investigation for the time being, pending, of course, the result of ours."

"Investigation of a drowning?" I asked. "What's going on here, Detective Anton? Is this a normal thing that the Sheriff's Department does, or is there something that you are not telling me?"

"No, Miss Martian, nothing," he countered. Then as if noticing for the first time my apparel, his eyes lingered on my neckline and he almost smiled. Self-consciously, I held my head up, clasped my robe tighter together with my free hand and looked straight into those hazel eyes and inquired if he would like to join me in a glass of wine.

"No, on duty," he replied. "Besides, I think you may be enjoying enough for the both of us." I began to take offense at the comment, but the way in which he said it and the twinkle in his eyes, simmered me down. I ventured to ask him then if he would like coffee, and he replied, "only if you would join me."

I brewed a pot of coffee while the detective enjoyed the view from my living room window; Chuck nuzzled at his side. He apparently liked animals, or was too deep in thought to notice for he stroked my dog's ears as he stood gazing at the lights shimmering beyond on the water.

Detective Anton commented, almost abstractly, that he thought my home rustic, yet very comfortable. Whether he was sincere in his statement or not, I replied that I enjoyed it as well, and that it had proved a safe, serene haven for me, until now. As I presented him with his cup of coffee and gestured toward the sofa (though he continued to stand), he answered almost ruefully, "Now Miss Martian, I think that the odds of having a death on the island, whatever the circumstances, is pretty darn good every 120 years. Don't you?"

N. R. De Witte

Chapter Six

I plopped down on the sofa my eyes wide and mouth open in surprise. He stood in front of me. "What do you mean, every 120 years?" I rallied, wishing silently that I hadn't given up my wine for coffee.

"Miss Martian, don't tell me you aren't aware of the infamous murder of island resident Peter Goutre back in 1875," he admonished. "A native, island-raised girl such as yourself?" His eyes twinkled. I wanted to smack him. He continued on with his history lesson, seeming to relish my discomfort.

"Well, part of all investigations encompasses past history. Being the history buff that I am I was aware of the episode 120 years back, though I did dig up the old records to refresh my memory." He sat on the edge of the sofa parallel to me and sipped his coffee. "It really is quite coincidental. It was *exactly* 120 years ago to the day, November 16, 1875. He sighed and looked at me and said, "I still can't believe you haven't heard the story."

"No, detective" I replied, somewhat snidely. "I haven't, but please continue. You have my full, rapt attention." I smiled sweetly, hopefully sickeningly so. This man was beginning to irritate me beyond belief, and I barely knew him.

"Very well. On this date 120 years ago, a French Canadian settler was murdered on this very island. He had settled here and established a homestead on the northwest side, around here I believe," (his eyes twinkled again as if he thought he was giving me a scare). "For about fifteen years, the settler lived a fairly secluded life. He did have a dog." Detective Anton looked pointedly at me. When I didn't take the bait, he continued, "Goutre had proved up his little homestead and had abundant livestock and an apple orchard. There was a rampant rumor that he had a treasure stashed away here. On November 16, 1875, there was a heavy storm, much like the one that hit yesterday. It toppled trees and damaged ships. When Goutre failed to keep his scheduled apple deliveries to buyers in Mukilteo, a concerned search party came over to the island to find out why. What they found was Goutre's dog, wildly pacing the beach. Goutre's home was vacant, with no evidence of burglary. Searching the grounds, one of the party members found Goutre lying dead amongst driftwood. A murder victim, he had been shot with buckshot, once in the chest and once in the head. Half of his face was blown away. The search party buried him up on one of the island's sand hills, not far from the cabin. Part of the island is rumored to be haunted, you know." he added. Pausing he repeated again as if I were a dunce or something, "I can't believe you've never heard this story before."

The words *blew away half his face*, skimmed across my mind and I reluctantly remembered my dream of the previous night. I cringed internally, but chose to ignore the detective's incredulous comment on my ignorance of island history and asked instead, "Did they ever find the murderer?"

"No, never did. Though rumor had it that two white men disguised as Indians shot him when he opened his cabin door. We'll never know for sure." He continued.

"Well, I'm sure that even though it is a coincidence that the murder occurred 120 years ago, the body in question today is just a drowning victim and not a murder victim such as the poor man described in your history lesson." I said the last words heatedly. I didn't want nor need a perfect stranger infringing on my life and giving me history lessons. "Now, is there anything else, detective?" I asked.

"Just a couple of questions. Do you walk the island every day?"

I replied, "yes, weather permitting."

He then asked, "Do residents around here know your routine?" I nodded yes, though I frowned as I did so. Who cared that I walked, and why ask? Though I didn't voice my questions, I wondered what he was driving at.

"Who or what are you hiding from?"

I stammered back at him, "What ever do you mean, hiding?"

"Well, I have to figure that an attractive woman as yourself must have some reason for locking herself away at a remote place such as this. Police record, or perhaps a love affair gone awry."

Steaming mad, I blustered back at him, "For your information, I've never even had a parking ticket. The other matter is none of your business."

He chuckled. "You're pretty cute when you get mad. I'll be

checking up on a police record, just in case. Not even a parking ticket, huh? Haven't had much fun, have you?" He seemed almost sympathetic.

Apparently satisfied with my answers or the fact that he successfully egged me on, Detective Anton handed me his empty mug and thanked me for the coffee. He said he was sailing with one of the Coast Guard cutters back to the mainland and had to get going. His eyes took on that mischievous twinkle as he said goodbye, but he did not smile. I was glad to see him go.

It was after I had let Detective Anton out the door and was in the kitchen rinsing his coffee cup that I reflected on the questions he asked. Though it still peeved me that he asked about my personal life, the whole encounter bothered me and made me a bit curious as to what was exactly going on. Sure, I had discovered the body, but that episode had been brief. What was the deal with the detective anyway? After all it was just an unfortunate accident, wasn't it?

Chapter Seven

Blessedly, I was suddenly tired (probably winding down from the liquor-high of earlier). Stocking the stove with wood, I turned off the light, closed the damper and headed for bed. The day had evidently been too much for Chuck as well, as he was already burrowed in blankets at the foot of my bed.

I didn't sleep well. Dreams of walking the beach and tripping over assorted carcasses amongst driftwood played as a slow moving picture in my subconscious. Waking up in a sweat, I saw the time was just after midnight. I was exceedingly thirsty, due of course to my earlier wine indulging. Getting out of bed, I put on my robe and went into the living area. There, in front of the main window, I wrapped my arms about myself and stared out into the night. Moon glistened radiance on the bay below, and stars twinkled in the sky. Blinking lights indicated various mainland activities from across at Whidbey Island. Everything seemed so peaceful and normal; however, not for many years since my divorce had I felt such a profound sense of loss. A feeling of total pain, and doubting of strength to continue living. I no longer relished my independence. I craved companionship. I wanted to be a more active part of the living. Did finding a dead body instill all of this in me? Was I really just a caricature in flesh myself, until now? Whatever the reasoning, I knew that I needed to start life again - wanted to start again; something that I had refused to acknowledge for the past couple of years. Perhaps the Detective had been right and I was hiding. Hiding from emotional ties and possible pain; from life and the chances one takes with it. I stepped into my small kitchen to grab a couple of aspirin and glass of water, after which I returned to bed and slept soundly, with no lingering dreams.

******

Awakened with a lousy headache despite my earlier aspirin, my mouth felt as though an army had marched through it. Why don't I ever learn? After letting Chuck out for his morning run, I went into the kitchen to make some coffee, and take more aspirin.

While my coffee was brewing, I showered and dressed. The shower made me feel a bit better, and I donned apparel much the same as yesterday's, though I hadn't the heart to wear my Scandinavian sweatshirt, perhaps for a long time to come. Instead I chose one that intoned, "Blessed Are Those That Drink Gourmet." Pouring my coffee and adding milk for just the right color and taste, I thought of my friend Gert. She constantly laughed at my coffee ritual, saying, "Why not have a little coffee with your milk?" Must be genetics, I mused, as my dad had drunk his coffee the same way.

At the thought of Gert, I pondered whether to call her at work. Gert was the head secretary and medical transcriber for the Snohomish County Coroner's office. I had known her for over five years, and considered her one of my closest friends. We had been school chums at the local college. She was there to get away from driving a school bus and increasingly obnoxious teenagers while I wanted to learn a trade to support my boys and myself after my divorce. Gert and I had formed a bond, camaraderie, and one that still stood. If there were any details to be had about yesterday's morbid event, Gert would be the one *in the know*, and would not hesitate to tell me.

I didn't call Gert. As curious as I was to know what had happened to the unfortunate victim, I didn't want to broach the subject just yet. It was still too raw, the visions too clear. Seeing a body versus transcribing surgeries and even autopsies differed dramatically. If something were amiss, Gert most likely would be the one to get hold of me. I'd wait patiently, as really there probably wasn't much to it at all. Little did I know.

N. R. De Witte

Chapter Eight

Carrying my steaming mug of coffee with me, I attempted to make some order out of my home. Straightening the bed, changing linens and dusting. I swept Chuck's hair from the pine floor and shook the colorful rag rugs that also seemed to have an abundance of those brown and white hairs. It was while I was shaking the rugs out on the slanted front porch that I noticed my Jeep. I mean *really* noticed my Jeep. The grounds around my home were virtually littered with tokens of the prior evening's storm. Except for my Jeep. Oddly it stood with no natural calling card on its exterior, yet the ground surrounding it was covered. Strange, I mused, at least I didn't have to worry about any scratches or dents. It would save me the time of brushing it off when I ventured off on one of my excursions to take the ferry mainland for a shopping expedition. Giving each rug an extra shake to rid it of all the dog hair, I went back into the warmth of the cabin.

"Patient is a wrestler and has had pain in his left knee for the last year or so. Originally began as a football injury while playing at the high school. He has pain at the medial and lateral joint line of his left knee. There is no instability, but some clicking and occasional snapping; no locking, but…" I rapidly tapped the keys, anxious to put at least a moderate dent in the mountain of transcription I needed to complete. After all, yesterday's events and proceeding storm had sadly put me behind in my work.

I was well into playing catch up with the transcription so I wasn't too annoyed when there was a knock on the cabin door, accompanied by Chuck' bark. Well, I reflected, the revolving door is starting early today. I hoped this wasn't a clue as to what would follow for rest of the day, as I still had scads of work to do, and didn't need distractions. However, I found upon opening my door that the new visitor was the best kind of distraction I could have thought possible.

Standing before me, on my slightly warped porch, was a man. What a man! Eyes an unsettling shade of gray with just the right amount of crinkles adorning their corners. Dark hair, almost black, with gray spiced at the temples. A nose that suggested a fist fight or two and a heart melting smile revealing even, white teeth. All features framing a strong face that spoke of intelligence.

I couldn't speak. I stood at the threshold with my mouth open. I could feel the warmth of embarrassment spread up my chest, neck and into my cheeks as I finally squeaked, "hello, could I help you?"

The Adonis spoke, in a deep, rich and truly masculine voice, and said "I understand you are one of the residents nearest to the marina with a working phone. The storm seems to have damaged the pay phone at the marina, and I wonder if I might use yours? I'll reimburse you for any charges, of course. By the way," as he held out his hand, "I suppose I should introduce myself, I'm Peter Cole." Again, he smiled and my heart melted.

I finally gathered my wits about me and introduced myself as well, ushering him to the phone located on the kitchen breakfast bar. "Help yourself," I stammered as he made his way across my recently swept pine floors to the phone.

Watching him covertly as not to appear nosy, I reflected how fortunate the island was to have phone service, provided by Whidbey Island Telephone Company. Years earlier, most phones were mounted out-of-doors on porches, sheds or any kind of protective overhang. Calls were made off hook via a central operator that manually handled all incoming and outgoing calls. I recalled the excitement when telephone technicians divulged on the island one summer, making the rounds from cabin to cabin installing inside lines and phones capable of direct dialing. And, now I sit here, on this very island 'downloading' material via the telephone to the mainland. In just a matter of years, the technological advancements have been astonishing.

I quit reminiscing and glanced again in Peter's direction. The weather had warmed up considerably, especially for November. Peter was wearing only a bulky fishnet sweater and worn, close-fitting blue jeans. I estimated that he was close to six feet tall, definitely proportionate to his weight.

Turning, as if sensing my inspection, he caught my eye and smiled. A dimple coursed the corner of his right cheek, and endearing quality. So was the absence of a wedding ring on his left hand.

Pulling my eyes away, somewhat guilty at being caught, I sauntered into the modest kitchen. Opening the compact fridge, I threw caution to the wind as well as my plans to complete my transcription and reached for an open bottle of Chardonnay. Perhaps I'd be cordial and offer him a glass. My nerves were on edge and I knew I could use one.

Peter didn't refuse my offer of a glass of wine. He seemed to be following my every movement as he spoke in low, rich tones into the phone. I was glad that I had dressed earlier as sometimes I would stay in my robe while transcribing, for the sake of comfort. I inwardly cringed thinking what a sight I would have been should I have opened the door to Peter with my old robe and "nursing home" hair.

Raising my wineglass in a subtle toast, I drank. Eyebrows raised, my guest made a closing comment and hung up the receiver. He took a large drink, swallowed, looked intently into my eyes and said, "Thank you, just what I needed."

"Do you have time to sit down?" I inquired, hopefully, motioning toward the adjoining living area where the wood stove crackling enticingly.

Peter replied congenially, "Sure, nothing much going on at the marina, especially now with all the havoc the storm has caused. Sort of has put everything in slow motion."

I nestled in my favorite worn rocking chair, absently crossing my legs. Smiling slightly, Peter sat across from me on the faded plaid sofa. Chuck immediately came to his side and placed a damp paw affectionately on his leg.

"Chuck, knock it off. Our guest doesn't want to hold your paw!" I admonished my pet. "It's okay," Peter interjected, "and I like dogs. How are you, fella?" He crooned, shaking Chuck's procured paw. I wondered if he was as good with humans as he was with dogs.

"Anyone who can put up with Chuck deserves a refill, how about it?" I inquired. Peter swallowed the remainder of his wine and handed me his glass.

Pouring the wine, I attempted light-hearted conversation. What brought him to the island, did he like it so far, did he golf? In my usual manner, I asked all these questions in one steady sentence giving him no opportunity to answer. Perhaps I should have.

Chapter Nine

Murmuring that indeed he liked the island, although he hadn't yet had the opportunity to explore it any farther than my place, and that he didn't golf, his attention returned to Chuck. I had approached him with the refilled wineglass and urged Chuck toward the cabin door so that I could be the one to have most of Peter's attention. I was successful in getting my pooch out the door, and gratefully closed it quickly behind him before he could change his mind.

Peter smiled as I sat back down in my rocker. "Now tell me Lily, is it? What do you do here on the island?" Looking around at the female furnishings of my small abode, he continued, "obviously quite alone?"

I told him about the move to the island and my current living circumstances (though Detective Anton's cutting remarks of the previous evening still stung in the background.) Peter glanced over at my computer terminal, and the papers scattered across the oak desk and seemed to be duly impressed, or perhaps it was just the wine.

I asked Peter what he did for a living. He smiled and replied that he was a research professor on sabbatical from Cal State. He had always heard about the beauty of the Puget Sound and until recently had never had the time or opportunity to explore. He had purchased a sailboat in Poulsbo, having numerous sailing lessons in California. It was time for him to "test his wings" so to speak and what better place than the wonders of western Washington islands. The storm, or warnings of it, had urged him into the Hat Island harbor and with graciousness seldom allotted strangers, Matt allowed him to stay until the storm blew over. Until the weather change, he had hoped to be on his way exploring Whidbey Island and the popular tourist attractions of the towns of Langley and Coupeville. His agenda was to go through Deception Pass and then farther north into the San Juan Islands to explore such treasures as Roche and Deer Harbors and beyond.

"Must be hard for a woman living here alone," Peter mused.

"No, not really," I said. Was he going to be one more man who thought women were weak? "I have my moments, but I have Chuck and a host friends. And," I added with a grin, "If things get too depressing, I could always take a quick dip in the bay to perk me right up." I inwardly hoped that my dimples were showing more than my age-induced wrinkles.

We chatted for a better part of an hour. I invited him to stay for lunch, but he declined.

"Thanks for the use of your phone and the wine. I'll be at the marina rigging the sailboat and determining storm damage for a few days, feel free to stop by." He smiled as he extended the invitation, gave me a wink and left out the door. I hung on the doorjamb and watched him as he sauntered down the drive, Chuck prancing at his side.

I sighed as I watched him walk round the bend, out of sight. Chuck returned to the cabin and I closed the door softly behind. Celibacy was not all that it was cracked up to be, and the bay was too far down the road for a quick cool-down session today. A cold shower would have to do the trick. I headed toward the bathroom, but only after grabbing what was left of the bottle of Chardonnay.

Infatuation must have dulled my senses as it wasn't until later, when laying in bed and scrutinizing the day's activities that I realized then how evasive Peter's earlier conversation, especially when he said, "not much happening on the island." With all the police and Coast Guard cutters milling about, that response had been utter nonsense. I couldn't imagine that he had missed the surplus of activity and should have picked up on it right away, but the man's good looks had certainly intrigued me and I overlooked common sense. Perhaps I needed to get to know Peter Cole just a bit more. And why not, he did offer an invitation for a visit. One I intended to take him up on, soon.

N. R. De Witte

Chapter Ten

Chuck's whimpering woke me. Evidently having a bad dream, as his little paws were moving as if he were chasing gulls. Gently, I called his name and scratched behind his ears in a subtle effort to wake him. Blood shot eyes opened and he looked around in mild confusion. Upon seeing me, he wagged his stub of a tail. "You're okay, fella," I whispered. He then settled back down and drifted back to sleep. I was content to lie abed and listen to the winter birds chirping at the nearby bird feeders as they sprinkled their meal of sunflower seeds to the ground. I let my mind wander and thought of having someone warm with me, other than Chuck. Actually, Peter's face came to mind almost at once, and I managed a wry smile. I wonder if he would bring me coffee in bed (only after passionate morning sex, of course). Cuddling further into the covers, I acknowledged, a girl does have dreams or in my case, fantasies.

Feeling slightly excited to escape the confines of my home and with the off chance I would bump into Peter Cole at the marina, I purposely dressed in new jeans, coordinating plaid shirt and buttoned my fleece-lined jacket. Stepping into sturdy boots, I shut the cabin door and planned my strategy of coercing Chuck for the umpteenth time into the shed (ala old outhouse), as I didn't need to worry about him at the Marina when I was searching out Mr. Cole.

As I made the trek to the marina, more evidence of the anger of the storm was present. I had not ventured this way since the storm, and now noticed the damage. The main road was littered on each side with branches and a large alder had apparently fallen across the road, but had since been sawed into small rounds and pulled to the side of the gravel road. Turning the bend and trudging down the hill toward the water, I could not help but notice that on a usually simple fall morning when scarcely a soul would be about, there were island residents as well as strangers milling on the marina dock. Curious, I approached a small pool of island locals seemingly huddled as if planning a great football feat.

"Excuse me, ah, Betty." I stammered, "what is going on around here?"

Betty Brummelman stood there with Leonard and Emma Jean Campbell and Captain Mike, skipper of the island's ferry, The Holiday. Deep in apparent conversation, Betty turned her piquant face to me and in almost a tone of conspiracy whispered, "Oh Lily, you don't know?"

Mutely, I gave a negative swish of my head. After which, Betty swiftly shoved in my hand section B of the local newspaper, with an article circled in red ink:

Body found on Puget Sound Beach Everett - The Snohomish County Sheriff's Office is Investigating the discovery Wednesday morning of a body On Hat Island beach.

The body, that of a male, and about 55 to 65 years of age, was discovered by an island resident on the Northeast side of the island. A preliminary identification has been made, but authorities are withholding information until all family members have been notified.

The Snohomish County Coroner's Office has scheduled an autopsy for Thursday morning. But the cause of death won't be known until test results come back from the Washington State Toxicology Lab.

I read the newspaper article, and then looked up questionably. With a dramatic sigh, Betty lifted her aged arms skyward and said with emphasis, "It was Sanford Wardell, Lily…. The dead man was *Sanford*!"

So much for my thoughts of the day before regarding checking to see how Sanford and Vivian had faired with the storm. Evidently, Sanford hadn't done so well. I can't say that I had any profound grief, just great surprise.

"Do they know what happened? How is Vivian…" Questions teemed from my lips, but Betty was already looking toward her approaching husband, Bob, in tow with their two Welsh Corgis, and did not answer my inquiry. The dogs' squat little bodies, with stubby legs, were skittering all over the dock - evidently excited at all the activity in their midst. Captain Mike had vanished, returning to the ferry for the trip to the mainland. This left me standing only with Leonard and Emma Jean.

The Campbells were a nice couple, recently retired from the Department of Health. They had been accepted warmly upon their move to the island and had joined with other locals participating in monthly pinochle games at the McPherson's on Section 4. Today, however, Leonard's lean face appeared pinched, and his intelligent blue eyes seemed almost frightened. Likewise, Emma Jean looked just as uncomfortable. Perhaps there were having second thoughts about having made the island their retirement retreat.

Before I could speak with Leonard and Emma Jean, however, I heard a voice from behind. "Good morning, Lily. Nice to see you again." I turned from the Campbells without hesitation and looked into the beautiful gray eyes of Peter Cole. Readily I accepted his coffee invitation and followed him along the dock, looking over my shoulder to see the Campbells looking after me with surprise on their faces.

Chapter Eleven

Peter guided me toward an immaculate schooner. Teak trimmed deck and portals glistened apparently from a new coat of tongue oil still wet from the looks of it. As if noticing my perusal, he remarked, "I'm attempting to fix her up a bit, storm damage and general cosmetic sprucing. Be careful getting onboard, it's still wet over there." He pointed to where I had been looking. Extending his palm, he deftly assisted me on board.

I sat down as directed by Peter on a cushy chair in the rear of the boat. The coffee must have been already brewing, for in a matter of seconds, Peter returned with two steaming mugs. Grateful for the warmth on the brisk November day, I wrapped by fingers eagerly around the mug. Taking a sip, however, I choked and stammered, "Irish coffee."

Peter smiled, did a mock toast and said, "How much better can it be, I have the sea, crisp blue sky and beautiful company."

Feeling my face grow hot, I shifted by eyes and murmured, "thank you."

"I'm sorry about that guy dying. I figure that this being such a small place, you knew him."

"Sanford was my neighbor. We weren't very good friends, as he and his wife didn't like Chuck too much. I am sorry, however, that he is dead. And, more than a little surprised. I'm glad to have run into you today, I feel better now."

Warmth was evident in his voice as he replied, "I'm glad to have helped. How's the coffee, need a refill?"

"Well, in a bit perhaps. What I would really like to do is have a tour of your boat. It looks fabulous!"

Peter was more than happy to oblige, and when we had both finished our coffee, invited me into the hold of the schooner. Giving me the guided tour, I properly oohed and aahed, which wasn't too hard to do as the schooner was as magnificent on the inside as the outside. Gleaming teak accentuated cabinets, floor and moldings. Plush fabric covered the small sofa which also served as seating for the adjoining compact table in the galley. Sturdy, spotless stainless encompassed the sink, fridge and stove area. Custom bookcases lined both sides of the seating area. Upon further inspection, I discovered that the entire bow was given over to a much too comfortable looking queen berth and built-in teak closets. A small, but solely functional bath, was tucked into a corner.

Naughty thoughts flitted in my mind (shame on me). Blushing I said,

"Boy, it sure is hot in here. Must be the coffee."

We returned to the upper deck and fresh air, though truth be known I would have rather stayed down below with him! On a second cup of coffee, Peter covered his travel itinerary with me, as well as repairs he needed to do to his boat before he set sail.

Abrupt tapping on wood and an "ahoy" interrupted Peter and I from further conversation. Matt tossed me a copy of the local paper over the sloop's railing. "Just thought you'd wanna know Lil', the body you found, it has been identified," he drawled, cigar stuck clenched in the side of his mouth. Giving Peter an appraising look, he turned back to me and continued, "Looks like its someone you know, heck, we all know. Sanford Wardell. Viv's not doing too well. Sorry thing tho can't say I liked the feller much."

Matt looked a bit disappointed when I informed him that Betty Brummelman had told me earlier about Sanford. However, I did say, "I guess I'm not as shocked now, when I think of it. Silver hair and all." Then I thought to myself, what was Sanford doing on that side of the island? Especially when his place was on the northwest tip, close to my own. The last few words of Matt's conversation brought me out of my pondering, "not giving out what happened yet, but I don't think it was a drownin."

N. R. De Witte

Chapter Twelve

Peter was silent during the exchange between Matt and me. Not much he could say since he hadn't known Sanford and was just visiting our little community.

Time seemed to fly and before I knew it, dusk would be just around the corner. I needed to free Chuck from the shed and perhaps check to see how Vivian Wardell was faring.

Thanking Peter for his hospitality, I left but not before agreeing to see him again the next day. I was humming to myself as I hurried out of the marina and up the gravel hill toward home. I wanted to get home and work more on my transcription so that I could really enjoy the following day with Peter. Also, I decided to bake a loaf of bread to take over to Vivian. As was customary in all cases of death and subsequent mourning, evidently it is thought that the loved ones left behind find comfort in food and strength to carry on. From past experience, however, I did not find this practice particularly true, remembering my own experience with my father's passing twenty years before. Food at that time had not alleviated any of the pain and misery and sometimes still the sight of a chocolate cake can stir up pain best left forgotten.

While the banana bread was baking, I sped through my transcription. "Patient has pain anteriorly in her shoulder once she does overhead work. She has trouble chopping wood, washing windows and activities of this sort." I guess so, I mused, rapidly typing up the notes.

I had just begun my next section of transcription and deeply engrossed in the world of sutures and splints when the phone rang shrilly (set of course to the highest of volumes for such occurrences.) Removing my headphones, I got up and crossed to the breakfast bar to answer it.

"Hello," I said. "Lil', what the hell is going on in that place?" Gert hollered, so much so that I had to hold the phone a good few inches away from my ear, either that or burst an eardrum.

"What do you mean?" I asked, though knowing about her position in the coroner's office, I believed I already knew what the basis of the phone call was. But why was she so upset?

"You know I can't breach conflict of interest, but you can certainly *GUESS* what happened to one of your little beach cronies over there...." She enticed.

"What do you mean, guess? He drowned, didn't he?" I countered, in an astonishing tone.

"Guess again, sweetie, you can do it, I know you can," she cajoled me along.

Aggravated, I gave in and said, "Okay, if he didn't drown, was he stabbed, shot, what?"

"No, but you're getting warmer, keep going," she invited.

Now, really getting bothered, and ever so curious, I said, "did someone hit him on the head?"

"Bingo!" She cried. "Only looks as if he fell off a cliff. His face and head are battered pretty badly. Died on impact Doc says. You know those large rocks in the area. Smashed his skull to smithereens. You can imagine, I'm sure." She continued, "You didn't hear this from me, by the way. Just watch yourself kid. Something funny is going on over there," she warned. "Oh, gotta go, Doc's on his way in." With that, Gert clicked off. I mutely stood there, phone clutched in my hand, though closer to my ear as her earlier shrillness had diminished, and wondering if what she said was true and knowing deep down it most certainly was.

****

In front of the fire nestled in my rocker, I pondered the fact that Sanford Wardell was dead. Apparent cause of death, cerebral trauma. It would indeed be interesting if the tox lab found anything in his body that would further implicate his death as a homicide. I knew that Gert would tell me if something were amiss. Otherwise, perhaps Sanford just plain fell off Chalk Cliff on the outskirts of Section H. But what was he doing there at Chalk Cliff anyway?

N. R. De Witte

Chapter Thirteen

The scent of freshly baked banana bread still wafted through my small cabin as I shrugged into my rain slicker. Securing the door behind me and with Chuck at my side, I trudged toward the Wardell's place. It was late in the afternoon, and I reflected on how the weather seemed to sympathize with death. On this solemn occasion, fog had sunk in enveloping within and around the island, emitting a sad, eerie atmosphere.

Though my home was near the Wardell's, the fog was becoming so dense that my travel was slower as I could not see but four to five feet of the road ahead. After what seemed an eternity and nerve-racking as well, I reached their doorstep.

Unlike my rustic abode, the Wardell's home was one of the island marvels. A magnificent Cape Cod complete with large front porch and inviting dormers. Standing on the doorstep and peering through the fog at the massive structure, I felt somewhat like a country bumpkin paying call to the rich landlords. Never the less, I promptly knocked on the lovely oak and leaded glass door.

I did not know who I expected to answer the door, certainly not Vivian, but was somewhat startled to see Betty Brummelman. Smiling at me, she placed her index finger to her lips in the certain gesture of "quiet," as if I was going to yell "howdy do..." or something. Signaling me inside, she turned and twittered softly, "So kind of you to come by. Poor Vivian is upstairs. Dr. Sorenson is attending to her. Such a shock, poor dear."

Handing the bread to Betty, I followed her ample, bright shape as she made her way across the gleaming wood floors into the expansive kitchen. Betty had changed from her usual island garb of jeans and sweatshirt to something she evidently deemed more appropriate for this sad occasion, a hot pink pantsuit. I was glad that I no longer had a hangover as the glare of her suit would have intensified my earlier headache.

Betty placed the bread on the kitchen counter. Looking around the room, I was struck by the loveliness of it. Ceramic tile counters and flooring shone under large recess lights. Gleaming stainless appliances winked as well. Oak cabinets line the L-shaped kitchen with a handy portable island perched in the center, and above on a pot rack hung gorgeous copper-based pots and pans. I watched Betty as she rearranged the food already laden on the counter. From the many cakes, pies and other breads as well as the heady aromas lingering in the kitchen of recently baked casseroles, I knew the island network was humming; catering and trying to convey sorrow at Sanford's death. Looking at the foods, I thought again about my dad's own *"after funeral" do.* Friends and relatives drinking coffee, chatting and eating. And, the ominous chocolate cake.

Betty interrupted my reminiscing by asking if I cared for some tea. I nodded and crossed to the breakfast table, pulled a seat and sat down, cautiously looking about in case she had brought her obnoxious dogs along. I wouldn't put it past Betty to bring them along, in the pretense of trying to "perk" up Vivian's spirits.

As Betty brewed the tea, I had a chance to scrutinize my surroundings. Vivian's home decorating taste was exquisite. Wall coverings of soft peach and teal gave the room a warm and inviting appeal. Peeking into the living room beyond, I could see the same color theme continued but with an added touch of beige.

Betty served the tea piping hot in des mode china teacups. Somehow, I wouldn't have had the nerve to use something as costly, mostly fearing "you break it, you buy it" theory.

Cookies of different shapes and sizes as well as quick breads, though not from my contribution, accompanied our tea time. Sitting down across from me, Betty explained that as far as she could tell, Vivian had no family, at least not here in Washington State. And, was still far too upset to even be considering funeral arrangements. Apparently Matt had finally taken the upper hand and had contacted a local funeral home in Everett to take over the arrangements, once of course, Sanford's body was released from police "custody."

Hearing approaching footsteps, I looked up as Dr. Sorenson entered the room. In his late sixties, lean and lanky, Dr. Sorenson was semi-retired. He and his wife lived in Langley, on Whidbey Island northwest of Hat. Weather permitting, and a powerful enough engine, a boat trip could be made in less than twenty minutes, which Dr. Sorenson often did as he was the island's self-appointed physician. Standing in front of Betty and me now, he hardly looked the part of physician. His sandy hair was mused, jeans badly wrinkled, with just a thin jacket and very smudged deck shoes. His eyes looked tired and his usual minimal wrinkles were extenuated. Nevertheless, seeing me sitting there at the table, Dr. Sorenson cheerfully smiled and stuck out his hand in greeting, "Lily, how are you?" His eyes were a warm gray beneath his wire frames. Taking his firm grasp in mine, I replied that I was doing all right.

Concerned masked Dr. Sorenson's face, however, and he ventured on, "Are you sure you are okay? I understand you found the body. That can be a very difficult and emotional trauma. Do not hesitate to let me know if you find that you are having trouble sleeping at night." I answered gratefully, and said that indeed if I did experience anything related, I would be sure to let him know. Dr. Sorenson smiled, and then shook his head as if curious. "Don't have the foggiest why Sanford was way over by Chalk Cliff. Did you see anything odd Lily?" I shook my head in denial, but did ask in doing so, "How is Vivian?"

Dr. Sorenson answered, "Physically she is fine, but

mentally, well… extremely distraught. I've given her some sleeping medication so she can at least get some rest. I'll stop back in tomorrow to check on her. Betty, could you or Lily stay the night? I don't think Vivian should be alone."

Betty and I both looked at each other, each questioning the other in blatant non-verbal communication. After a long pause, and when Betty's eye contact broke away, I volunteered to stay the night with Vivian. A look of gratitude and relief appeared on his face, as well as on Betty's, though her look was mostly that of relief. Betty offered Dr. Sorenson some tea, but he declined stating that he needed to head back home since the fog was so thick and had to navigate by his

GPS. Looking self-consciously at me, Betty excused herself to walk Dr. Sorenson to the door. Angrily, I took a big slurp of hot tea, and burned the roof of my mouth, which only incited me more. I was mostly mad at myself for getting suckered into staying the night. Perhaps Betty felt that since I was single, I had no one to be with anyway.

After all, she had Bob. Regardless of reasoning, I much preferred my own home and bed but I would put my glumness aside and do the neighborly thing as well as that of being a good island resident, I would Vivian-sit.

Chapter Fourteen

I hurried home through the mist. Less than three hours to finish my transcription, tidy up the cabin and pack a few things for overnight detail at Vivian's. I had noticed how Betty had avoided direct eye contact with me when she had returned from walking Dr. Sorenson to the door, and well she should have I fumed.

Chuck and I entered the dryness and warmth of the cabin and I was hit again with despair of having to stay away from my home, even for one night. The place had become my own little haven and I was seldom away except for few and far between vacations with my sons to Ocean Shores or the occasional stay at Gert's such as the approaching Thanksgiving holiday. Chuck seemed to discern my temperament and whined at my feet. I bent and stroked his back, explaining that he would be on his own and in charge of the home front for the night. With that, I checked for phone messages, opened a can of soup (an increasingly steady diet) and heated my dinner in the microwave. While the soup bubbled, I poured myself a glass of Chardonnay. I'll sip and type I mused, perhaps my inner fuming will stop.

I was able to complete my transcription much sooner than I had anticipated. Most of the minutes involved classic family practice visits, and thankfully no long, detailed prognosis or introductory letters to other physicians. After cleaning up the cabin, mostly the kitchen resulting from a hasty early dinner, I packed a few things in my overnight bag; underwear, toothbrush, hairbrush, soap and face cream. In addition, I could not forget my pillow. I could not, nor would not, ever sleep on another individual's pillow and for years had been carting mine around with me from place to place when staying elsewhere. I'm quite certain that I made quite a sight sometimes.

Securing the cabin with a confused Chuck inside, I headed back to the Wardell's for my overnight duty. Betty was planning to stay until I arrived in order to let me in and to allow poor Vivian continued rest. Though I seriously doubted that she could have awakened from her drug induced slumber had she wanted to. Betty opened the door once again at my knock. And once again, she motioned quiet with her finger to her lips. I was becoming increasingly annoyed by her manner, but bit back a retort and squeezed a tight smile as I nodded yes. Though giving into childish behavior, I did stick out my tongue at her retreating back as we headed once again toward the kitchen.

"Casseroles and salads are in the fridge," she explained, "so feel free to help yourself. I'm sure there will be plenty of food for the guests after the funeral…whenever that may be." Well, I reflected, at least I could peruse the pantry in peace with Betty gone. One small comfort to look forward to. Betty quietly chatted albeit nervously and avoiding my eyes, as she put on her coat and grabbed her handbag. She literally hustled toward the door, as if I would stop her at any given moment and demand that she stay so that I could leave. I watched her flit out the door. Peeking out the adjacent window, I saw her scurrying down the drive as if in pursuit waving her flashlight in front of her. I stepped back, sighed, and locked the door.

In the midst of my elegant meal of assorted casseroles and fresh salads, I remembered that I had left my trusty pillow on the bench by the cabin door. Shoveling a last bite of Chinese hamburger into my mouth, I hurriedly got up to check on Vivian. A brief check to make certain she was still snoozing away and I could dash home and retrieve my pillow. I crept up the stairs to locate a sleeping Vivian.

The upstairs was vast, and I had never had the privilege of being in this part of the Wardell's home. From the many doors that lined the corridor, I had to peek into each one to find Vivian. Though being the somewhat "curious" person I am, really didn't mind. As with the downstairs, the furnishings upstairs were just as grand. Imagine all this luxury on my little island. Who would have thought? I spied at least two guest rooms, complete with matching furniture and bedroom ensembles, a large bath and separate sitting area. I located Vivian at the end of the hall when I opened the last door. There she was, ensconced in a four-poster as big as my kitchen, which I guess isn't really saying much. Luckily, I did not have to turn on a light as the fog had begun to lift and moonlight filtered through the large window at the right of the bed. I crept up silently to Vivian.

"Vivian, it's Lily. Are you awake?" I whispered softly, hoping she was still in la la land as I didn't want to deal with any hysterical weeping (not that I'm not sympathetic, but fearing I'd join in). I could hear her even breathing as I approached the monstrosity of a bed. Vivian lay supine, amidst the blankets. Her usual elegant coif didn't look so elegant now. Tufts of definitely dyed hair jetted out from unusual angles around her pointed head. She had indeed been weeping, as mascara had stained the areas underneath her eyes, leaving them dark and bagging with her aged wrinkles in full force. Smudges of bright lipstick creased her mouth and spiraled down her jaw. She looked like hell. I felt like hell standing there perusing her. Visions of her all of sudden opening her eyes and seeing me just inches away urged me to back up a bit and slowly turn to leave the room. Before I got more than a couple of steps, however, I saw the bottle on the nearby night stand. Tiptoeing, I edged close to the night stand and picked it up. Under the light of the moon, I read the prescription. As an experienced transcriptionist, I knew that the medication in my hand would keep Vivian asleep for several hours. No doubt Dr. Sorenson had given her this powerful drug not only for its prescribed anti-depressant agent, but for it strong sleep-induced side effect as well. From the large count left in the bottle, I summarized that he anticipated Vivian taking it for some time to come. As I left the room, I once again looked at Vivian and felt a great pang of pity. In her twilight years and now alone. Not much to look forward to now.

I rinsed my dinner plate, wiped off the small table where I had dined on the feast of funeral foods. Turning off the kitchen light, I grabbed my coat, and edged out the front door closing it softly behind me. After donning my coat, I flicked on the small flashlight stowed earlier in my pocket. Thankfully the fog had lifted, so navigating by the little flashlight, along with moonlight glow, I made for home. Since Detective Anton's history lesson about the gruesome murder 120 years before, my active imagination could conjure up anything, including Peter Goutre's ghost. Therefore, my rapid steps took me home far quicker than usual.

Matt had evidently been at the cabin as he had left the Friday paper on the porch. Presumably, he had picked up an extra paper from Mike Shaw when the ferry had come over on its 6:30 evening run from the mainland. Placing the paper under my arm, I unlocked and opened the cabin door.

A thrilled Chuck greeted me. Snuggling close and licking my hands as I made my way to the breakfast bar, he was indeed glad to see me. I marveled at the unconditional love of an animal, most specifically that of a dog. "Sorry boy, but I won't be staying long," I crooned at him, feeling guilty leaving my pet behind. As if he could understand, I continued to explain, "have to go back and stay with Vivian, just grabbing my pillow for the night." As an after thought, I selected a chilled bottle of Chardonnay from the fridge, then a favorite book, Agatha Christie's, "The Mirror Cracked," and stowing my pillow under my arm began to leave my home once again. I was just securing the lock when the phone rang. Deciding whether to answer it or not, I decided to fight my way back into the house and awkwardly made my way to the phone. Putting my things down, I breathlessly answered, "Hello."

"How come you always seem to sound out of breath when you answer the phone?" Inquired Gert, then she continued on with barely a breath, "You up to something?"

I muttered back into the receiver, "I wish, er, I mean, hardly."

Gert sighed, "yeah, sure; I know what you mean. What are you doing anyway? I called to see if you want to come over to the land of the living this weekend. Joe and Kelly are going to her soccer tournament tomorrow in Olympia, and I'm going to be all by my lonesome. We can go to dinner, catch a movie, you name it." She sounded wheedling to me.

"Sorry, Gert, can't. I've lots of work here to do, with the activity and all; I have things I need to catch up with. Anyway, I'm going to spend Thanksgiving with you as planned next week, so perhaps I'll be able to take an extra day and we can shop the big after Thanksgiving sale." I didn't like invoking a little white lie especially to my good friend Gert, but I did have a few things that needed to be done and quite honestly

I was hoping to spend much of the day with Peter.

Not at all surprised by my decision to stay home, Gert replied warmly, "Okay then, but be careful. I will be glad when those tox tests come back from the state lab. Doc says victim's injuries look pretty suspicious. Got clobbered a big one on the back of his head, Doc found several wood splinters. He feels strongly it was prior to the other injuries…. something about coagulated blood in the tissues. I know I'll be typing the lingo soon enough." She trailed off while finishing her sentence as if in deep thought. "Anyway, call me tomorrow, okay?" And clicked off the line.

Strange, I thought, she sure seems concerned about something. All these years she had been razzing me about living on the island and that I should be living on the mainland, safe and sound. Ha, if anyone anywhere is safe and sound in this day and age no matter where you happen to live.

I could hear Chuck whining from within the cabin as I left. The wine, paper and trusty pillow secured under my left arm, I guided the tiny flashlight with my free hand and hurriedly dashed back to the Wardell's.

Letting myself back into the house, I removed muddy shoes. For some reason, my drive had been muddier than usual and since I hadn't taken the jeep out for a week or so, figured Matt and the island bus must have churned up the drive by bringing me the paper. Taking my things back into the kitchen, I flipped on the light and crossed to place my wine in the fridge to keep cold. Unenthusiastically, I knew I had to go back upstairs and check on Vivian again.

N. R. De Witte

Chapter Fifteen

I crept stealthily back up to the second floor and was just about to the door of Vivian's room when I noticed a dark stain on the corridor carpet. Bending down, I inspected and determined that it was mud. Irritated, I concluded that I must have tracked mud onto the carpet the last time I was here. I had tried to be so careful then. Darn, I'd have to go in search of some carpet cleaner after I checked on Vivian. I could just imagine Betty Brummelman admonishing me about my careless ways. Good thing I removed my shoes this time around.

The door was slightly ajar. Pushing it further open, I could see Vivian still in the big bed, presumably still in deep slumber. Wishing not to disturb her, I shut the door and went in search of the cleaning solution.

Luckily, a good solvent cleaner was under the kitchen cabinet. Grabbing a dishcloth, I hurried back up the stairs and was able to remove most of the stain. Hopefully Vivian would not notice the small smudge in her present state of despair. After putting away the cleaning supplies, I uncorked my chilled bottle of wine and poured some into an ornate crystal flute I had spied in Vivian's china hutch. Well, I reasoned, if Betty Brummelman could use priceless china, I certainly could use crystal stemware! Taking my glass to the breakfast table, I plopped down and opened the paper Matt had left at the cabin. Noting the usual world news, mostly about a new crisis, or for that matter, continuing ones, I scanned the rest of the paper until I reached Section B, local region news. There, on the front page, was the article I was looking for:

Body Found to be Resident of Hat Island

Everett - The body of a man found on the southwest tip of Hat Island beach Thursday was identified Friday as that of Sanford G. Wardell, 67, resident of the island.

The Snohomish County coroner ruled that Wardell died of multiple traumas to the head. While the coroner has not ruled on whether the death was accidental, suicide or homicide. "At this time we have no reason to believe foul play was involved. It is believed Mr. Wardell fell from Chalk Cliff to his death accidentally. Though toxicology tests are still pending." Commented homicide Detective Nick Anton.

Wardell, originally from California, had lived on the island for just over

> **one year. He was active in
> the community and was
> retired from the banking
> industry. He leaves his
> wife, Vivian, at their
> island residence.**

Reading the article made everything so much more real. In my mind's eye, I saw the seaweed entangled hair and twisted body of Sanford. And, only one shoe. Morbidly I ached again for a sleeping Vivian. Looking around, I thought *what a shame*, such a lovely place, an ideal retirement locale and no one to share it with.

Folding the paper and pushing it aside, I sat back and sipped my wine. I felt alone and missed chatting with Peter. Brightening a bit, I wondered if I could persuade him tomorrow morning to take a trip to the mainland. Perhaps he needed supplies for his boat due to the storm damage. Smiling, I mentally selected my wardrobe and planned my method of attack. I refilled my glass from the wine bottle, and ventured into the plush Wardell living room. It was far lovelier than the brief peek I had earlier.

Beautiful sofa and loveseat in fine brocade with glass tables artfully arranged nearby. The furniture ensemble was arranged to take full advantage of the large windows capturing the gorgeous views of sea and sky. Expensive artwork graced the walls and, on closer inspection, I noted that they were painted by one of the area's most noted seascape artists. Framed photographs sat atop the carved oak mantel of the large stone fireplace, which graced the east wall. Photos of a smiling Sanford and Vivian no doubt taken on special occasions or vacations. One picture was especially lovely captured in an ornate, gold frame. Sanford and Vivian looking year's younger posed smiling with another man, one who looked familiar but one I couldn't place. With sadness I helped myself to a large chug of wine.

I didn't want to sleep upstairs where Vivian was, as I felt much more comfortable downstairs. I could use a couple of quilts I spied earlier in one of the upstairs bedrooms and along with my pillow, and could sleep on the living room sofa. I crept back up the stairs, but instead of opening Vivian's bedroom door all the way, I listened for any sign of movement with the door ajar. Noting none, I was satisfied that her drug-induced sleep would carry her further on into the night and turned to nab the quilts in the nearby room.

Situating the sofa downstairs was easy and I quickly stripped to my bra and panties. It was fairly warm in the Wardell home; most likely due to the large propane furnace system Sanford had installed when he built the house. I enjoyed the comfort of the continuous warmth as I crawled underneath my procured quilts and settled myself. Taking up my mystery book, I plumped the pillow and adjusted the light on the adjacent lamp. Turning to a page where I had left off began to read....

The whistling and howling of November wind awoke me with a start. I looked around trying to regain my faculties as to where I was. Straightening, and easing my neck from its awkward position, I picked up my book from the floor where it had fallen and turned off the nearby lamp. Plumping my pillow behind me,

I gazed out the window at the trees, which were casting shadows against the adjacent wall. Between the whirling and humming of the wind and the graceful swing of the branches dancing in the shadows, I thought about the story Detective Anton had told me. I had always felt so safe on the island, now my vivid imagination could and most likely would think up all kinds of scenarios of Sanford Wardell's death as well as the ominous one that had occurred 120 year ago involving Peter Goutre. I made a mental note to ask Matt about the Goutre murder as soon as the opportunity arose - the entire event fascinated me (though I wouldn't let Detective Anton know). The correlation of deaths *exactly* 120 years to the month and day was uncanny. Hoping that was all that was similar.

Late fall sun peeked through the large living room windows, casting glare on my face. Scrunched onto my side, I tried to avoid the brightness, as I wanted to snooze just a bit longer. Unfortunately, my substitute bed wasn't very comfortable and I could not get back into the sleeping mode. I threw back the quilts and got up to dress. Once again I was thankful that the Wardell's did not skimp on their heating, the large home was still as comfortable as the night before, despite the chill of fall weather.

After brushing my teeth, running a wet comb through my tousled blonde hair and dressing in sweater and jeans, I headed to the kitchen to peruse for coffee. While the coffee dripped, I went to check on Vivian. The kitchen clock showed 7:45 AM, so perhaps she was awake by now. Looking through the crack in Vivian's bedroom door, I could see clearly in the morning light that she was still resting in the big bed. Not wishing to disturb her, I headed back downstairs to start breakfast. Perhaps the scent of cooking would make their way and slowly rouse Vivian from her sleep, though secretly I wished she would slumber on as I wasn't quite ready to neither pacify nor cope with her despair.

Good thing I'm not a big eater, as all there was in the massive kitchen was shredded wheat cereal (yuck), egg beaters (double yuck) and "just starting to turn" wheat bread. Though there was still the array of funeral foods, I was somewhat reluctant to help myself once again, as I did not want to incur the wrath of Betty Brummelman lest she had counted each and every crumb. Mollified with the coffee, I sat and waited for Betty's early morning arrival and the *changing of the guard*, so to speak.

Admitting Betty in the front door moments later, I noticed she was much more relaxed and even smiled at me and inquired if I had had a good night's sleep. In addition, she asked about Vivian. No wonder she looked better, having slept in her own bed last night. My back still ached as I tried to place a congenial smile on my face and answered her questions.

"Well, I would have slept better at home, naturally," I began, "but I did fine. Vivian has been asleep since Dr. Sorenson left last night. The drug he gave her is quite potent. I checked on her about twenty minutes ago."

"You brewed coffee. Good. I dashed out of the house this morning after getting Bob his breakfast and didn't have time to catch a cup for myself," Betty said this while heading for the kitchen. Couldn't Bob prepare his own breakfast? What happened to women's lib? Men certainly were not helpless creatures, though thinking about past relationships noted that some were. A man that was self-sufficient and a true partner in all senses was my ideal.

Thinking of this, Peter came to mind and I thought of his hospitality the day before. I wonder what else he is good at. I aimed to find out.

Betty was busy having her coffee and meandering through the fridge, most likely looking for breakfast staples or taking an inventory of what I had helped myself to. While Betty perused in apparent delight with oohs and ahhs echoing through the hallway and into the living area, I gathered my things from the night before. I was anxious to head home and rescue Chuck from the cabin and also plan my strategy of urging Peter to accompany me to the mainland for the day.

N. R. De Witte

Chapter Sixteen

I dashed home through the fall morning sun, stripped off my clothes and stepped into a steaming shower. I had let Chuck out to do his duty and chase the fall birds. He had maintained the home front splendidly and needed time to run. Also, he would be locked up again soon enough when I headed for the marina and, hopefully, a trip to town with Peter by my side. Lathering my short hair, I thought of the impending trip. Peter may not only need supplies for his sloop, but maybe I could coerce him into lunch at Anthony's Homeport Restaurant.

The restaurant is situated southwest of the Everett Marina, one of the largest marinas on the West Coast. With views of the Port of Everett and surrounding moored vessels, only accentuates the restaurants wonderful culinary offerings. Perhaps if we arrived early enough, we could secure a window seat and enjoy a glass of wine as well as each other's company. My little brain was just teeming with plans….something that I shouldn't do to myself since I've experienced more than enough of disappointment in the past.

Having concluded my shower, a bit longer than usual but so worth it, I towel dried, and slathered moisturizer all over my body as the salt water breeze, along with fall/winter weather, was havoc on one's skin. Besides, I smiled, I wanted to look soft and supple to Peter. Just in case.

Scrutinizing myself in the mirror, I had to admit that I looked good. Matching lavender sweater and leggings accentuated the green of my eyes. I applied mousse to my blonde hair and after drying it, fluffed it up a bit more than usual. Liberally I applied blusher, eye shadow and deep plum lipstick. Tucking perfume behind each ear and between my breasts, I knew I not only looked good but smelled good as well. Looking good was for my own benefit as well as for Peter's. I enjoyed looking good for my own self-esteem, though to be truthful turning the opposite sex heads' never hurt either.

In the living area I checked my recorder, since I had been in too much of a hurry to clean up to check it when I had got home. I was both thankful and relieved that there were no messages. Having set the automatic transmit unit for the transcription last night before I left for Vivian's, my work had been electronically wired to the clinic on schedule. Today was my free day, and I was going to enjoy it! Grabbing my jacket and purse I headed out the door.

Urging Chuck into the shed was more difficult than usual. He was getting far too wise to the process. Finally, I had to toss in a couple of hot dogs. He may be wising up, but his appetite still ruled.

Heading toward the marina, I was pleased to see that the sun still held and the wind was only slightly breezy. As my mom used to say, the bay looked "flat as a pancake." Fall and winter months sometimes prove to be calmer seas than that of blustery hot summer days. And indeed this was a calm day. Our ferry trip would be smooth and quick.

Rambling down the ramp to the dock below, I could see the Holiday had already begun loading her passengers for the 10:00 AM run. Since I didn't see Peter, I headed toward the "Sea Mist" to see if he was there. I was apprehensive, and butterflies were skittering in my stomach as I approached the sloop. As if sensing my presence, Peter emerged from the galley hatch and secured it behind him. Turning he smiled, hoisted himself over the side and walked the few feet to my side.

As he approached, I stared at his dark hair and hazel eyes.

Longingly, I wished I could mold myself to his body. I felt an immense urge to be with him and realized that my self-imposed celibacy had been a bit too long. I was not a wanton woman and was a bit miffed at myself for the sexual arousal Peter's presence gave me. Was I now trying to make up for all the years of loneliness? When a brief caress was all I could expect, when Friday night sex was quick and unsatisfying.

"Hello Lily." Peter's voice broke into my scattering thoughts. "Glad to see you. You sure look good today…if I may say so. How about a cup of coffee?"

"Coffee would be great, but I was wondering if you needed anything from the mainland. I could use a few things and I thought, if you weren't too busy, that you might be interested in joining me for a day over at Everett. The ferry is boarding now." I said all this so rapidly, I wondered if he could decipher what I had asked. My face felt hot, and I knew I was blushing.

Peter laughed, either at my stammering or red face, perhaps both. "Well, I do need some things, and luckily made up a list last night. Let me grab it and a coat and I'll meet you by the ferry."

Smiling smugly I turned to make my way toward the ferry, but didn't get far before Matt was in my path. He scowled at me, and looked me up and down.

"You look like the cat that got the dern canary…an' where you off to, lookin' like that. Goin to some party? Haven't seen you so dolled up since last New Year's." If he was expecting an answer, he didn't give me time, but continued on, "talkin to that pretty fella I see. He goin with you to Everett?"

I bristled at Matt's comments and insinuation, and replied, "Yes, Peter and I are going to Everett. He needs supplies for his boat and I need a few things as well. Also, though I don't have to explain anything to you, I dress up every now and then, so it is no big deal. I can't look like a beach bum all of the time. Now, if you'll excuse me,

I'm going to get us a seat." I brushed past him and rapidly walked away. I was angry. I didn't like him questioning me and making comments on what I looked like. Glancing over my shoulder, however, I could see the alarm and a touch of hurt on his face. More than likely he was just concerned about me. After all, neither one of us knew Peter and Matt was most likely being just a friend. Albeit an annoying one.

"What's wrong with the old guy? He just gave me a glare that could kill," laughed Peter as he approached me by the ferry stairs. "A bit jealous from the looks of it, if you asked me."

"Oh, I don't think he is jealous, not at all! He is just concerned. We are a fairly guarded community here on the island and all watch out for each other. He is just doing what is natural that's all," I explained this to Peter, but I really didn't believe it myself. Matt could be a real butt a times. He had no reason to be apprehensive about me spending the day with Peter, or did he?

N. R. De Witte

Chapter Seventeen

We boarded the little ferry. Formally a 42-foot tug boat, that had been refurbished nearly 30 years earlier for passenger ferry service to the island. Passenger fare used to be dirt cheap, but with the current market of fuel and general upkeep the price had increased substantially. For me, and others like me, it was still far cheaper than mooring a boat at the marina, paying slip fee, insurance and fuel besides. And there was something relaxing about boarding the ferry, not worrying even as five foot swells or more splashed the bow because the sturdy vessel was sea worthy as well as trust worthy.

As anticipated, we could choose from any seat we wished, as the ferry was only accommodating a handful of passengers this morning. Les and Emma Jean Campbell were on board in addition to Sam and Dorothy Hansen from Section G east of the marina. With the addition of Peter and myself, the little Holiday would indeed have a light load.

Captain Mike Shaw, with the help of one of his numerous adolescent grandchildren, fluently pulled away from the dock and headed out of the marina. As the sky was clear, so the waters remained as well. We cruised at the usual 10 knots smoothly through the silver sparkles toward the Everett waterfront. Peter and I had decided to sit downstairs in the ferry rather than up above due to the briskness of the fall wind. Pleasantly, we looked out the side windows and enjoyed the scenery of green waters, gulls, and occasional glimpse of seals peeking above the waves. As we passed the inland marker buoy, two enormous sea lions sat resting on its bobbing surface. They leisurely looked at us as we passed, but had no fear for they were used to the perusal of boaters and seemed to enjoy the attention. At least that's what I thought as they certainly did not move one inch of their massive bodies and looked at us in benign pose.

"Terrible thing that happened to Sanford Wardell," Les Campbell's voice broke me away from the mesmerizing bay view. Looking up, I frowned and shook my head in agreement.

"Yes, very sad. I stayed with Vivian last night, but was not able to talk to her. Dr. Sorenson had given her some sleeping medication, and it really did the trick. She slept all night and into this morning. Betty was with her when I left." By this time Emma Jean had approached from her seat at the front of the boat. She and Les habitually sat directly three rows behind the captain. She had evidently heard the tail end of my conversation with Les, as she didn't ask any further questions about Vivian. Emma Jean smiled sweetly and hooked her arm through that of her husband's then looked inquiring over at Peter. Clearing my throat, I introduced him to both Les and Emma Jean. Peter scored more points with me, as he braced himself against the listing of the tug, stood and shook hands with both the Campbells.

"Pleased to meet you. I'm just visiting your little island paradise, and my friend Lily has invited me to explore a bit of Everett scenery with her. As well as get some supplies for my boat." He seemed so natural and at ease. I could very well imagine him at the college lectern dutifully instructing his students.

Les, however, did not want to relinquish the commiserating regarding the Wardell's as he said, "Well, it's just a darn shame. We're on our way into town to get her some flowers. Not much one can do really, but perhaps it will let her know that we are thinking of her. Well, have a good day. Nice to meet you Peter."

Emma Jean chimed in, "Yes, very nice to meet a friend of Lily's. See you on the 4:00 o'clock return!"

Smiling, arm and arm, they lurched back to their accustomed seat.

Smiling, I waved a little "bye bye" and was pleased indeed when Peter placed his arm about my shoulders, though casually, it was a wonderful feeling none the less. He commented, "Nice people. Friendly, down to earth. You're lucky to have such good friends and neighbors."

I hadn't really thought about the Campbells that much since they were so new to the island, but Peter was right they were nice people and the island community was certainly fortunate to have them. I then made a mental note to purchase flowers as well. My piteous banana bread was a poor token of condolence, especially among splendid casserole dishes, exotic cookies and extravagant bouquets of posies.

As is usual on a nice day, the Everett boat launch where the ferry had a space for disembarkation was teeming with activity. Fishermen were busy loading or unloading their boats and kite flyers were rapidly descending on the grounds beyond to enjoy the brisk wind. Because of frequent northwest showers, western Washingtonians take advantage of clear weather whenever possible.

After leaving the ferry, Peter and I walked up the cement dock toward the parking lot, passing several mid-morning crabbers and fisherperson's trying their luck from the edges of the dock. We walked across the gravel parking lot to my old Honda Civic parked at the end of one of the many rows. The car was a bit grimy, but other than that seemed to be in the same shape as I had left it two weeks prior. Unlocking the doors, Peter and I climbed inside. The car started almost immediately, and we traveled through the drive out onto the asphalt, dodging trailer and boats emerging from the ramps.

Peter asked, "What area is this again, Lily? It's a pretty busy place from the looks of it."

Laughing, I replied, "This is the Everett boat launch and you should see it during the summer if you think this is busy. Lines of boats waiting to be unloaded. I don't have the patience for it myself, and am glad I can use the ferry, even though the fare keeps increasing. Moorage is available over at the Port of Everett, the main marina, but it is expensive and there is quite a wait to get a slip." I was rambling I knew, but was so excited to be with him that I just continued on, "The marina is great, with shops, a terrific hotel and a couple of good restaurants. We can have lunch there now, if you'd like - before the mad noon day rush." Looking at his watch, Peter said that seemed fine as it was just past 11:00 o'clock.

We drove to our lunch destination, skirting the edge of the Everett Naval Base, which abutted the marina. Parking nearby the restaurant of choice, Anthony's Homeport, we entered the restaurant and were pleased that the early hour afforded us quick seating as well as a window view accommodation. Our cozy table overlooked the guest mooring dock facing west. In fact, and I pointed this out to Peter, we also faced Hat Island and could discern the many homes as well as marina from where we sat.

"Sure looks close, doesn't it?" Peter exclaimed.

"Yes, as if a person could almost swim to it. It seems so close, yet when I'm there it's as if I'm a world away. I murmured as I leaned on my hands, elbows ensconced on the table edge. "My uncle told me that as a young adult he and friends used to row right over there," I pointed toward the south tip of the island, "where they would purchase homebrew. I can't really imagine that, to tell you the truth, it must have been some calm waters."

"When young, you feel indestructible, you remember that don't you? Your uncle was just lucky he didn't get hurt or drown. But the island itself, you really love it, I can tell." Peter's statement didn't invite argument. He could tell my feelings about the island even though he'd only known me for a couple of days.

"Yes, I love it. Totally. I've never been so content in my life. I'm only missing a few things." I said this, almost wistfully.

"Such as…" Peter urged.

Just at that moment, *in the nick of time, saved by the bell*, the waitress approached to take our beverage order. We ordered Chardonnay. Two brimming glasses were brought to our table along with a steaming basket of hot, sliced sourdough bread. Between bites of crusty bread and sips of wine, sort of a religious experience, we perused the menu. Meal selection always has been most difficult for me as there is so much to choose from and all of it sounds good. Being on a continuous diet, and not wanting anything too heavy, I decided on Spinach Salad.

Peter, however, seemed to be just as indecisive as I was. "What do you recommend, Lily?" He queried, scrunching his brows in deep concentration.

"Well, my favorite is the seafood fettuccine, but the hot seafood salad is good and so is the clam chowder." I dutifully filled him in on my favorites of the restaurant.

Peter snapped shut the menu and stated, "That settles it, seafood fettuccine. Is that what you are having too?"

With a negative shake of my head, I replied, "Nope, not today. Have to go light and just have a spinach salad. I'll just watch you and try not to drool."

Taking up his glass for a sip of wine, he said, "If you're a good girl, I'll let you have a taste."

"Gee, you're kind. I'll try and be a "good girl." I'd hate to ask what I needed to be or do should I want a bite of your dessert." I was teasing him, with definite sexual overtones. Lily, I silently told myself, don't bite off more than you can chew, especially with a virtual stranger. As if I had a good fairy on one shoulder and the devil on the other, my inner thoughts then countered with, "Why not go for it! You're lonely, deserving of some fine male companionship, what can it hurt?" "Lots" my good angel on the left said, "keep your head." No wonder I never had much fun, I've always listened to the good angel.

Peter's voice broke the debate going on in my brain, "Hello in there, you look a million miles away."

I stammered and then pointed, "I'm sorry, just day-dreaming. Look out there that's the Mosquito Fleet ferry. It does specialty runs as well as ferries people back and forth to Jetty Island, which" I turned slightly to my right and pointed, "is over there."

Yachts were tied at the nearby dock with For Sale signs bobbing up and down in their windows as if enticing future buyers. The area between the restaurant and the dock was given over to salmon spawning. Black wire cages under the salt held the promising fish, growing and developing for an eventual short life span in the bay beyond.

While staring out the window, I noticed the Coast Guard cutter usually moored a couple of docks over, rapidly advancing out of the marina to the river inlet. Not abiding to the "no wake" zone regulation, the cutter sped rapidly up the river toward the opening bay beyond.

"Wonder what's going on with the Coast Guard," I said this to Peter while following the cutter with my eyes as it turned right at the end of the rock quarry and headed out to sea.

"Hard to believe it would be anything bad. Such a nice, calm day and all. Now relax, and let's toast to a good day." Peter lifted his glass to mine and we toasted.

But I was not be put off, "One death on the island is enough. More than enough. We've had our flurry of activity now its time to get back to normal. The detective on the case, Anton is his name, stopped by my place the other night. It was kind of odd, instead of more questions, he ended up reciting an island murder that had occurred exactly 120 years to the day."

Peter perked up, "Murder, 120 years ago you say? Now that's interesting. What did he say about it?

"Just that the victim was an island homesteader rumored to have a cache of loot hidden somewhere, though nothing was ever found. Only his poor dog knew what happened and of course couldn't tell. I'm going to ask Matt what he knows the next time I have a chance. It's kind of neat really, guess I never thought about much island activity any earlier than the mid 1900's. I ended my statement by washing down my bread with a sip of the cool Chardonnay. I could almost forgo my lunch entree and feast on the bread and wine.

Any further speculation into the Goutre murder or even Sanford Wardell's was squashed as the waitress arrived with our lunch.

Watching Peter dip into his fettuccine, I wished for the umpteenth time that my metabolic rate was faster, either that or I was three inches taller, enough to evenly spread the weight around. Even though my salad was attractive and tasted good, it wasn't as good as the steaming pasta liberally laced with scallops, crab, large bay shrimp, and cod which sat directly across the table from me. I could almost taste each delectable bite.

Looking at me, Peter laughed and said, "Lily everything you are feeling is written all over your face." Smiling, Peter spooned over a generous portion of his fettuccine onto my bread plate.

Lunch was leisurely; we watched as the restaurant rapidly filled with patrons. Our timing had been perfect. Hectic waiters and waitresses rushed around trying their best to accommodate the onslaught of customers. Plates banged, glasses clinked while we relaxed. I hadn't had such fun and good company since I could remember.

When the waitress finally got a breather, she returned to ask if we wished dessert and I decided no longer to torment myself. I ordered the dessert special, Cherry Buckle. We finished our lunch with steaming cups of coffee and sharing the dessert. Each submersing our spoons into the heavenly tart. At one point, Peter fed me from his spoon and I did likewise with mine. My loins grew warm just with that small act of sensuousness. The day had started well and would only get better as far as I was concerned. How could it not?

N. R. De Witte

Chapter Eighteen

Leaving the restaurant, Peter and I headed toward Everett for supplies. Since I needed to check my post office box, we decided to make the post office our first stop, then on to the grocery store and finally ending back at the Port for purchase of Peter's supplies at the local marine supply store just south of the boat launch.

I urged the Honda up the precipitous hill on Pacific Avenue and turned right on to Colby to emerge on the one-way street bordering the large post office. Parking, Peter and I entered the double door.

Mail had jammed my little post office box, and I had to pry it out. Thumbing through the stack, I noticed that the boys had sent me something (most likely a cash request) from school, the phone bill, electric bill and car insurance renewal were also included which certainly can take the fun out of the day. However, I had a letter from my cousin Rose who resides in Seattle. I smiled as I viewed the envelope which was decorated with Rose's curlicue handwriting and drawing of a rosebud next to her return address. Rose steadfastly refused to use e-mail, stating that since she had to fix telephone equipment that supplies the stuff, she wasn't having any more of it than she had to. I smiled when I thought of her. Very similar in looks to me, Rose and I were kindred spirits. We often laughed that it was a good thing our mothers (sisters) liked floral better than fauna or else would have likely been named Bunny or Bambi. Smiling again, I imagined the rosebuds being a bunny or even that of a baby deer. Stuffing my mail into the side of my purse, I turned toward Peter.

He was rubbing his head as if weary. I asked him what was wrong and he said he had a headache and wondered if there was a pharmacy near the grocery store I was headed for. I assured him that the store had an on-site pharmacy. As we pulled into the parking lot, I glanced at Peter and noted he did not look well. His face was ashen and sweat beaded his brow. Smiling slightly, he emerged from the car and called over his shoulder that he would meet me somewhere in the aisles. I watched him rapidly make for the entrance to the store and head back toward the vicinity of the pharmacy.

I was a bit worried. Hopefully, it wasn't the lunch. He had seemed so well this morning and during lunch. I ruminated a bit as I delved over and over again to what he had eaten. Between my selection of fresh vegetables from the produce department, as well as fruits, I was convinced that he had a case of food poisoning. Worriedly I strolled up the aisles, filling my cart with essential non-perishables of crackers, canned soup and a few toiletries. Heading over to the wine section, I perused my favorites looking for sales, and thus selecting a couple of bottles of Chardonnay. Over at the tiny garden section, I was able to find a lovely European flower basket for Vivian. Deep purple violets peeked out amidst deep green feathered leaves. A touch of white mum, a sprig of ivy and a quaint silken bird dressed the basket. Glad that the Campbell's had mentioned their intention as I probably would have not thought of the gesture on my own until too late. One of the detriments of living on the island is that a trip to the store was indeed a *trip*.

I was relieved to see Peter stride up the aisle toward me, tucking something into his jacket pocket. His color was better as were evidently his spirits. I smelled the spicy chrysanthemum, and looking up commented, "You look better."

He sighed, ran his hand through his hair, and replied, "I'm fine. Don't know what got into me. I think my blood sugar got a bit whacked out. But, I'm good to go now. How are you doing, got everything you need?"

Blood sugar. I thought about that remark. I hadn't noticed anything about him to warrant diabetes, and I shouldn't jump to conclusions but the medical transcriber in me was already secretly diagnosing him. Smiling I linked my arm with his and pushed the cart toward the nearest available check stand.

After loading the groceries into the Honda's trunk we headed back toward the marina to purchase Peter's supplies.

The Crow's Nest was open for business. While Peter was guided amongst the nets, buoys, ropes and whatnot by a hopeful salesclerk, I browsed through the books and t-shirts located at the entry. Though I loved boating, I wasn't too enthused with all the paraphernalia that went with it. I limited my enthusiasm to colorful calendars, books or nautical apparel.

The schooner must have been in more ill repair than I had thought for Peter had a large box of supplies. Paint, lacquers, sealants and etc., peeked out from the box. I could only hope that the bulk of the supplies meant that the "Sea Mist" was in for quite an overhaul, thus having her skipper at the island a little longer than originally planned.

We stowed the supplies in the Honda's trunk and I was thankful that for a compact car it had a trunk large enough to accommodate a substantial amount of cargo. On several occasions the trusty car had transported items of various size for my island retreat. Another hour remained until it was time to return to the ferry. Peter and I decided to take a few bread slices from my newly purchased loaf and feed the ducks at the launch.

We sat together on the wood bench that graced the nearby walkway. Tossing crumbs to the ducks and observing as they quacked and waddled toward their feast, trying desperately to outrun the hovering gulls above. A few times, a brave gull would dive, thwarting a duck's slow attempt to nab the bread. We laughed; the fall sun was beating down upon us, the green water beyond was rippling in the mild breeze and nature was at our feet. It was turning out just like I had hoped, a perfect day. *Little did I know.*

N. R. De Witte

Chapter Nineteen

Les and Emma Jean walked past us to board the ferry. Glancing at my watch, I noticed that we had about fifteen minutes to gather up our supplies and board for our journey home. Tossing the remaining crumbs, Peter and I gathered our purchases and carrying them carefully along the dock, boarded the small ferry.

The wind had picked up a bit, and our ride was through much more choppy waters than earlier in the day, though the tiny tug plowed right through the ominous waves. White caps danced along side the tug and the fall sun, dimmer now because of descending evening, glinted on a wave now and then. Peter sat beside me, arm casually thrown around my shoulders. I missed this endearment. It made me feel protected, almost cherished. I was glad to have an active imagination.

I had brought my flower basket inside the hold with me, as the rest of the cargo was out back on the storage area of the ferry. Even though there was only a handful of passengers, there was a fairly hefty cargo load.

Les and Emma Jean smiled as they made their way back to their original seating behind Captain Mike. Emma Jean followed my train of thought, and had brought her potted plant in doors as well.

Our trip was relatively short, despite the churning seas. Usually, I am a bit anxious to get back to the island and the last 15 minutes seem like an eternity, however, today I could have cruised to Timbuktu and back and it still most likely wouldn't have been long enough. I owed this feeling to being with Peter and not wanting to part company with him any time soon.

Captain Mike docked the Holiday as efficiently as ever and in no time we were clamoring to gather our belongings and exit the ferry. It was at that moment that I remembered that I should have driven my jeep to the marina in order to bring my purchases home. A hike up the hill with two large, heavy bags was too difficult. Well, I figured, guess I'll leave the sacks at the marina office, walk home, relieve Chuck and drive the jeep back down to get my stuff.

Peter was busy hauling his box over the side of the ferry and hoisting it up to take over to the schooner. I followed him and explained that I would return with the jeep in order to get my things in a bit. "Just a sec, Lily, I'll help you carry the stuff up the ramp." He offered.

I waited at the end of the dock. It was at that time I noticed the Coast Guard cutter moored on one of the inside slips. Wariness seeped through me. Why was the Coast Guard here again? Trying not to panic, I searched the area above the marina for Matt or another island resident to ask; however, dusk was fast encroaching and visibility was limited. I knew I needed to start home while there was still a bit of light available.

"All set?" Peter inquired as he approached my side.

"Look, Peter, there's the Coast Guard cutter. Looks like it came here after all. Wonder what's going on now?" I said, with an edge to my voice.

"Probably nothing, or perhaps continuing their investigation of Wardell's death. You worry too much." He calmly intoned.

"I know I worry. But Detective Anton said that it was a police matter now and that the Coast Guard was out of it. And there's no one about to ask." I still searched the area above me for signs of someone to query, but only saw Lee and one of his brunette girlfriends loading golf supplies into his pickup. He was too far up the hill to yell at, and I didn't want to jog up the ramp and dash across the parking to ask him. He'd probably think I had the hots for him or something.

"Come on Lily," Peter cajoled, "Let's get this stuff of yours up the ramp, I think I can get a few things done before it gets too dark, and you'd better hit the road for home."

No sooner than we had placed my purchases near the tiny marina office, Peter bent down and kissed my cheek and said that he would stop by the cabin later in the evening, if it was okay. I was inwardly thrilled, but managed a warm, yet controlled smile and said a visit would be fine.

I hiked the short distance back to the cabin. Letting Chuck out of the shed, I watched as he danced and jigged around the yard, taking pit stops along the way. Poor boy, such a good sport. He hasn't been this confined for quite some time.

I was just unlocking the cabin door when I noticed a white business card stuck in the door jamb.

Inspecting it, I saw the name Detective Nick Anton, Snohomish County Sheriff's Department, Homicide Squad. With a sinking feeling, I wondered what Detective Anton was up to now and when I could expect him to return.

Chapter Twenty

Only one message light was on my recorder, and it was Gert. Her high pitched, agitated voice filled the room as she blurted, "What the hell is going on there anyway? Give me a call pronto!" a loud click followed as if she slammed her phone down on the cradle. Dismayed I looked at the phone in my hand. I don't know what's going on. Is something? I could picture Gert in my mind's eye, squeezing the phone as if in a vise, her iron curls jiggling, bifocals perched part-way down her nose and furiously chewing on a plastic coffee stirrer. Vacillating between calling back or returning to the marina, I decided on the latter. I wasn't up to a verbal encounter with Gert at the moment, why ruin the day?

Chuck seemed reluctant to approach me as I closed the cabin door. No doubt thinking that I would place him in the confines of the small shed again.

"Not to worry, pet. I'll leave you outside. I'm just heading down to the marina to get my things." I reassured him, though in that mournful spaniel fashion, he looked rather uncertain.

The jeep was certainly grimy. I cringed thinking that soon I'd have to get the car soap, finagle with the hose and give it a wash. The boys were so helpful when they were at home, washing the vehicle at a moment's notice. Though in reality, they were hoping to give the rig a spin, to aid in drying off, of course. Wiping leaves from the windshield, I bent down to retrieve the key from the top of the driver's side tire. It was not there. Feeling around the ground in case it may have fallen, I still could not locate it. Perplexed, I sat back on my heels and thought if I might have unconsciously moved it to another tire. Sometimes, I'm on automatic pilot, and don't pay attention to what I may be doing. Rising up, I went around to the passenger's side, and ran my hand over the rim of that tire as well. Eureka! My hand brushed the keys. I clasped them, stood up and went to unlock the jeep's door, thinking to myself as I did that I was sure I placed the keys on the driver's side tire, I always did.

Climbing into the jeep, I sat and had to adjust the driver's seat. I either had shrunk, or the seat had been adjusted. Perhaps I had a more bulky coat on the last time I drove. Wondering, I turned the key and the jeep roared to life. Downshifting, I rattled down the drive, Chuck loping alongside, and headed back to the Marina and my purchases.

Maneuvering into the loading area beside the small office, I could see the top of Matt's hat through the small paned window. Popping the rear door, I exited the jeep and went to get my purchases, which were still sitting next to the office. It was dark and I was glad of the marina lights.

"Whoa there, Lily. Wher've you been? Been lookin' for you. Did you hear…." Matt drawled.

"Remember, I went to Everett with Peter today, Matt, and got back a while ago. Came to get my stuff. Gotta rush and get these groceries up to the house." With that, I picked up my first sack to place it in the back of the jeep. The marina lamp was shining directly into the back of my jeep. My usually empty rear compartment was not empty, however. I stared and seemed to lose the strength in my legs. Sagging against the side of the jeep, I pointed into my vehicle.

"Lil', what is it?" Matt inquired, with some alarm, he had evidently followed me from the marina office.

"Yes, Ms. Martin" came the unexpected voice of Detective Anton. "What's the problem?"

Mutely, I turned in both their general direction, pointing again to

the back of my jeep and answered
breathlessly, "A shoe."

N. R. De Witte

Chapter Twenty-One

"Please step away from the jeep Ms. Martin." Commanded the authoritative voice of Detective Anton. "Sergeant Reed, over here please. Bring the print kit with you." He said this over his shoulder to a young officer, who looked both uncertain and wary. His red hair was in contest with his freckles standing out against his white face, which fairly glowed in the lamp light. I watched as he approached, donning rubber gloves as he neared my vehicle. Taking up kit, with brush and powder, he looked over the situation and laboriously began to dust.

Detective Anton brought me out of my mesmerized stance of watching the young officer turning the back of my jeep into a talcum powder mess. "Ms. Martin, are you aware that Vivian Wardell was found dead today? Reportedly, just after you had left her. Mrs. Brummelman found her." He peered at me over his bifocals and I noticed again his hazel eyes.

I must have looked ashen, as he then gestured me toward a seat adjacent to the office. Sitting down, I tried to think coherently. Evidently Vivian wasn't sleeping the entire time I was at her house; I felt sick.

"Ms. Martin, are you okay? You look a bit green about the gills." Detective Anton had squatted down on his heels and was peering up at me, intently. He certainly was an intent man.

"What happened, Detective" I whispered.

"I was hoping you could tell me." He replied.

Wearily, I rubbed my hand across my forehead, and said in a dejected tone, "I don't know what's going on any more. I did check on Vivian, and when I did, she was still alive."

Detective Anton, as if sensing my demeanor, seemed to lighten up. Ms. Martin, are you comfortable enough? I have quite a few questions to ask and I think it best to speak in private, at your place."

How Matt kept his mouth shut this long, I did not know. Though he was quite enthralled with watching the fingerprint ministrations. Turning, he made to approach me, but I put up a hand to warn him off. I did not need him interfering. I couldn't cope just now lest he got over protective and loud.

Detective Anton picked up a couple of sacks of my purchases. Rising, I picked up the now worthless floral basket and remaining sack. We walked single file over to the used school bus, Matt following quietly to drive us back to my place. It was a slow, silent ride.

N. R. De Witte

Chapter Twenty-Two

Chuck was happy to see me and my entourage. He assaulted Detective Anton with curious sniffing and licks and followed closely at our heels as we approached the cabin. Matt had dropped us off without a word, sensing my demeanor, I'm sure.

"It's open." I said softly. For I hadn't locked the door since I had planned on returning right away. Opening the door and pushing it wide, Detective Anton stepped aside to let me into the cabin first. Apparently, he had gentlemanly traits.

175

We set the sacks on the kitchen counter and I placed the basket of flowers on the window seal of the breakfast nook. Ignoring the detective, I began to unload the groceries.

"Ms. Martin, we need to talk." He seemed stern, and continued on, "Your prints were found all over the Wardell home and on the medicine bottle. Why is it, Ms. Martin, that you keep turning up around dead bodies? And now there is the discovery of a mysterious shoe in your jeep. interesting if it is Wardell's missing shoe."

I could feel myself getting angry, confused, and extremely frightened all at the same time. I had done nothing wrong. Sure, I had discovered the first body, whose wife died while in my care, and now whose shoe may have turned up in my jeep - but I had done nothing wrong…. The enormity of the situation pounded in my head. My little haven of heaven was becoming a den of hell.

While Detective Anton watched me, I placed my newly purchased bottles of wine in the pantry. Then, I marched over to the compact fridge, whipped out the opened bottle of Chardonnay I had brought back from Vivian's, uncorked it and took a deep swig. At Detective Anton's uplifted brow, I defiantly took another. "I'd offer you a glass of wine Detective, but you're on duty." I smiled at him, though it was a mirthless one.

"Ms. Martin, I believe that you may drink too much. I suppose that there is nothing much else to do here on your island. Cooped up alone, and with your dog no less." He mumbled this, almost to himself, but I caught the statement.

Bristling, I replied heatedly. "Detective, what I do is none of your business. I have a good life here. Unfortunately, the last few days have gone to hell in a hand-basket, so to speak." I uttered these last few words feebly, and moved to sit down on the breakfast bar stool. I placed my head in my hands, shoulders slumped in a pose of self-defeat.

"Let's sort this out, shall we, Ms. Martin? Perhaps you can fill me in on your night at the Wardell's. What time you checked Mrs. Wardell, if there were any visitors.." He seemed to invite my diction.

I replied in a monotone mumble, as I still held my head in my hands. "No one came over, if that's what you mean. Dr. Sorenson had given Vivian something just before I got there. When I returned, about three hours later to stay, Betty said that she was still sleeping. I even went upstairs to check on her. She WAS breathing. It was then that I picked up the bottle to see what he had given her. The bottle was FULL." I said this rather emphatically.

"So no one came by, and you didn't leave?" He questioned.

"No, no one. And I was there all night. I even have a sore back to prove it. I…" A light went on in my head, but it seemed so inconsequential…really nothing to further embarrass myself in front of Detective Anton, again.

"Well, what is it Ms. Martin?" Probed the detective.

Reluctantly I said, "It's just that, well, I did go back to my place for just a few minutes. I had forgotten my pillow." I could have sworn he smirked. "I wasn't gone but, twenty minutes or so." I trailed off sheepishly. Remorse set in. What if whatever happened to Vivian had occurred while I had been gone? It had been my duty to stay with her. I blew it.

"Could you have been gone perhaps longer, say an hour?" Queried the detective.

"No, I was only gone a short time. I did receive a call when I was home, but kept it very brief. I'm sure you can check the phone records." I remarked, snidely.

"I may just do that." He retorted. "So, you left Mrs. Wardell, went home for a bit, returned and did not bother to go and check on her again?"

"I checked on her when I got back. But I only looked through the open door and did not get close enough to see if she was breathing. Everything seemed fine to me - nothing was out of place and no one was about." Something gnawed at the back of my mind, something I had noticed when I had returned. Of course! The mud. Perhaps I hadn't been the one to track it in after all, perhaps someone had come in after I had left - what if that someone had killed Vivian?

Chapter Twenty-Three

Taking a more polite swallow of wine, I relayed to Detective Anton my suspicion about the mud on the Wardell's carpet. The carpet I so conveniently cleaned. With my stroke of luck, I had probably ruined vital evidence.

"Ms. Martin, are you with me?" Detective Anton attempted to rouse me out of my self-circumspection. "About what time was this?"

"I don't remember. I didn't think to check. Maybe 7:00 or 7:30 PM, I can't be sure. I suppose if you really do check my phone bill, you can add another fifteen minutes to it, that would give you a close enough time." I shuddered. Vivian may have been dead then, or the killer could have still been in that house. It was large enough. One could probably hide anywhere. God, I'd even gotten undressed and he could have seen me! Ugh. I had been visualizing Peter Goutre's ghost, not knowing that a real-life ghoul might have been but inches away.

"Well, we will know after the preliminary autopsy report comes in." Continued the detective. "Right now, we are treating this as a suspicious death. Could have been the lady woke up, was so distraught over her husband's death that she over-dosed. Still, it doesn't answer the question of that shoe in your car." He smiled. Why in the world would a man smile over something as sinister as this. Did he get his kicks this way? Probably. He seems the type, I thought crossly.

Just to be spiteful, I lifted my head and replied hotly, "It's a truck, not a car. And, I haven't used it for well over two weeks. In fact, I couldn't find the key at first, it was hidden in the wrong place. I thought I might have done that subconsciously, but now I'm not so sure. Also, the seat was adjusted for someone of another height. I think someone has used my jeep."

"Well, if that's the case, then perhaps he or she left prints. Sergeant Reed is dusting, if there's a good set of prints, he'll pick them up." Detective Anton, spoke while jotting down the information I had relayed in his ever-present, trusty spiral notebook.

"How well did you know the Wardell's, Ms. Martin." He asked.

"Not too well. They were rather elusive. Stuck up to be exact. I always wondered why they lived here when from the looks of it, they would have been more happy at some posh retirement community or resort. They did not socialize here, just dress up and go to town every Wednesday. And, as you must have noticed, their home is something else." I ended with, "I didn't harm either one of them detective, and I'm as puzzled as you. Maybe more so."

"Most suspects, and I'm afraid you are one Ms. Martin, I would tell not to leave town. In this case, I'll instruct you not to leave the island." With that last cryptic comment, he shut his notebook, clicked his pen, and got up to leave.

I took another swig from my bottle. I would be in fine shape when Peter arrived later. I wondered if he had seen any of the activity earlier at the Marina? Though it was so dark by the time I had returned, I doubted it. I'm sure he would have ventured over to see what the trouble was. The thought of him, and pending visit was comforting. I needed far more than a hug at this point.

I must have dozed, for a knock on the cabin door and Chuck's simultaneous bark awoke me. I remembered that after the Detective had left, I had put the wine away, and crawled on top of the sofa, pulling a quilt on top of me. Emotional exhaustion must have taken over, for I did not recall anything until the tapping at the door.

Getting up from the couch, I glanced at the clock, which read 8:52 PM on the illuminated dial. He was late. Though it did not matter. Perhaps earlier I would have been worse company than now.

At the door, I called. "Who is there?"

"Lily, it's me. Let me in, it's cold." Peter spoke hastily, as if the cold had already seeped into his bones.

I unlocked and opened the door. Peter rushed in. Closing the door softly behind me, I watched as he tossed his jacket across the back of the bar stool and made for the fire to warm his hands.

"Detective Anton was here today, Peter. Vivian Wardell is dead. I think he believes I'm involved some how." I could feel my throat tighten, and tears pricked behind my eyes. I'm usually quite stoic, but now felt less and less sure of myself.

"The lady's dead?" Peter was incredulous as he turned to look at me while in a squat position still warming his hands. "I saw the activity at the marina, but was so wrapped up working on the Sea Mist, that I really didn't pay too much attention. Your old friend was following the police everywhere. Probably trying to help them solve their case." He chuckled, but at my forlorn look, sobered and said, "Why do they suspect you? That's crazy."

"I know it's nuts. Everything is just now." I looked intently at him. The need for comfort was apparent. All the fear, anger, frustration and lust I had within me now brimmed in my eyes. We stared at each other briefly, silently giving and receiving the message. He rose to meet me as I crossed the room. I tore at his clothes, he peeled off mine. In the light of the fire, I straddled him and stared deep into his eyes, urging him to keep me safe, to take me to another world far, far away. He did.

Chapter Twenty-Four

Peter had left during the night, or wee hours of the morning. I was so exhausted from the emotional strain of the day before (and evening), that I apparently had snoozed through his departure. Though I did wonder upon waking and finding him gone, why he felt he had needed to leave. Perhaps he was unsure of my appearance in the morning? Hah! That must have been it. After the hair sticks up (nursing home hair my sons used to say) and the make-up rubs off, I doubt if even the world's most glamorous model would look appealing. Sadly though, morning was my favorite time. A time to wake leisurely, make love to your partner, thus giving the day a great "jump start."

Sighing, I rolled out of bed, shoved my feet into moccasins and put on my robe. Shuffling into the kitchen, I ground beans for coffee and looked out the window to ascertain the day. Sundays were always my favorite. For years my mainland ritual had been to rise, make breakfast for the kids and taxi them to Sunday School. I would enjoy coffee with the rest of the moms and sometimes stay for the last morning service. All this while my husband snoozed in bed. Though to give him credit, he did put in a full day's work at the store. Coming home from Church with the kids in tow, I would be able to sit down and peruse the Sunday paper, taking in the happenings of the week and the multitude of advertisements. Even now at my island home, Sunday was somewhat still a pattern. Though I could not attend Church, unless I stayed over at Gert's, I still made my coffee and while it brewed, dashed down to the marina to intercept Captain Mike for a Sunday paper. He brought an armload back on his return from the 9:00 AM morning run to the mainland. I would then drink my coffee, study the paper, and glimpse out at the bay. Depending on the weather, I'd tidy up and Chuck and I would head out for a walk.

Today was no exception. While the coffee brewed, instead of dashing for the paper, I showered (just in case I bumped into Peter). After dressing, and sprucing up, I poured myself a cup of coffee and decided to walk to the marina for the paper (since my jeep was indisposed). It was 9:20 AM, and I knew the ferry would be pulling into the dock in short order.

Sipping my coffee from my travel mug, I took my time walking to the marina. Whether it was just because I was still tired or reluctant to encounter prying eyes, I wasn't sure. Chuck loped beside me. The weather was a lot like yesterday's, still rather mild for November. Winter birds chirped merrily in the trees. My mind was trying to block the horrendous events of the previous day, but as I crunched along the gravel, passing the Wardell's home, it came back in swift abandon. Imagining Sanford's corpse as well as that of Vivian's raced through my mine. A lump arose in my throat. The fear and frustration of all the previous days began to enfold once again.

I don't remember the walk down the hill to the marina. I was so absorbed with my thoughts of the Wardell's that I was already at the marina office before I realized it. Matt's voice entered my subconscious. "Lil', lookin bit peaked this mornin'. Wanna come in and sit down?" He queried.

Looking at him, I could see the concern in his rheumy blue eyes. I gave a half-hearted smile and replied. "I'd like that, thanks."

Matt had a small portable heater operating in the small office. It was warm and cozy and I felt relieved to be there with him. He sat at his make-shift desk, filtering through papers, patiently waiting for me to speak.

"I don't understand what has been happening the past few days,

Matt. Have the police said anything to you?" I quietly asked him, misery etched on my face.

"Nah, not really. I think they're as stumped as you. Sanford's death was real puzzling, and now Viv's. Though she mitta done herself in. But, Lil', what was that shoe doin' in your jeep? That's what looks so strange…." He looked intently at me, hoping for answers.

I had none, but cleared my throat and met his eyes. "I truly don't know, Matt. I believe, however, that someone used my jeep to haul Sanford's body over to Chalk Cliff and to push it off, trying to make it look like an accident. Must be someone from the island, otherwise, how would he or she know about my keys, or for that matter, Chalk Cliff?"

"Don't know, Lil'. Why Sanford Wardell anyway? The whole things a bit confusin', that's for sure." He picked up his coffee mug, chipped and stained, lifted it to his lips for a drink. "Want some coffee, Lil'?" He politely asked.

191

"No thanks, Matt. I've got a whole pot waiting for me at home. Just came to get the Sunday paper. Matt, I know you were making arrangements for Sanford's funeral, did you come across any relatives? We'll need to know especially now with Vivian gone."

"Wardell's got a brother in southern California. The police were going to try and get 'hold of him. Looks like he'll have to come up and take care of the house and belongin's. Hope he's not as stuck up as Sanford." He grimaced as he took another sip of coffee. "Sure you don't want some?"

Not after that grimace I sure didn't. "No, thanks. Got to get going." Getting to my feet, I patted my thigh to indicate to Chuck (sleeping at Matt's feet) to follow me out the door. At the threshold, however, I stopped and turned. "Matt, there is something I wanted to ask you. It's about Peter Goutre, the frenchman that once lived on the island, you know, the murder back 120 years ago."

"Well now." Matt scratched his chin. "That's for sure. Interestin' thing, that French Peter thing. That's what they called him, you know. French Peter. Though the injuns called him "Stu-hy," a nickname earned through years of hard bargaining. Guess whenever the injuns asked for money for their goods, good ole' French Peter would reply, "Too high, it's too high." He chuckled. "Quite a fellow from what I've heard. Lived on a long spit of land southwest of the old sawmill that was on the Tulalip Bay cove. Tribes called it "Skayu Point", which meant ghost or dead soul. Injuns kinda were a feared of ole' Goutre, living there all alone, in their ancestor's resting ground."

Matt leaned back on his chair, seemingly searching for more information to divulge. I did not say anything, but waited for him to continue as I was extremely interested in this new bit of island history.

After a few minutes, Matt continued. "The territorial governor, Stevens was his name, signed a treaty setting aside part of that Tulalip site for the reservation. Folks homesteading there had to leave, which included French Peter. Most went to Whidbey or Camano Island, but not French Peter. No sir, that's when he came here, to the island. Government paid all the homesteaders a certain price for their land. It has been told that Goutre got about two thousand dollars. Quite a haul in them days, and that's probably why folks were always talkin' 'bout his hoard of gold. Though the government didn't pay off in gold, but greenbacks. Yeah, French Peter had it pretty good. Lived here on the island, 'bout fifteen years or so. Every so often he'd head over to Mukilteo in his row boat for supplies or 'cause he was dry and lonely. Got a bit mean legend had it, when he drank. Lotsa jealousy too. Goutre, miser than he was, had his apple orchard, lots of livestock, and made it through bad times lot easier than other folk. Think it caused lotsa hard feelins'. Maybe that's why he was done in. Don't know. Interestin, huh?" He chuckled, again, revealing his cigar-browned teeth. He laughed loudly then, causing me to jump and Chuck to growl. "Ya know Lily, ol'

Goutre lived about where you do now. Kinda scary, ain't it?"

Scary wasn't the word I had for it. Bizarre was more like it. I didn't verbalize my thought but said instead, "Thanks Matt, for the talk. Gotta go." Urging Chuck out the door and the warmth of the small office, I left Matt still chuckling to himself over the outrageousness of Peter Goutre and his life of yesteryear.

N. R. De Witte

Chapter Twenty-Five

The ferry had docked while I had been talking to Matt. Any passengers that had been on the refurbished tug this fall day had quickly dispersed upon landing. Therefore, I was able to walk quickly and unencumbered to the ferry to find Captain Mike and the morning paper. He was in the back, securing the lines off port side.

"Mornin' Lily, came for the paper I see." His merry green eyes twinkled. With his sandy hair and ruddy complexion, I envisioned he looked just like his Irish forefathers. Captain Mike handed me the Sunday paper over the rail, but when I went to grab it, held it tight and looked me straight in the eye.

"Don't worry about anything. We all know you had nothing to do with what has happened. The police will figure that out soon enough. Keep smiling." He had just released the paper and stepped back, when Lee Treasure bounded up to my left side, seemingly out of breath. (He reminded me of an over-eager puppy.)

"Hey, guys" He panted. "I think I left my clubs on board, mind if I take a look, Mike?" He asked, all the while looking at me. I looked back, and took in his breathlessness, as well as his apparel. Lee was so spruced up he looked as to join the winter PGA Tournament. That, or else he was posing for some Golf Magazine.

"No, not at all, Lee. Go ahead. I was just telling Lily here that we all know she had nothing to do with what's been happening."

Lee turned back to me, as he was headed toward the stern to look for his clubs in the storage area.

Meeting my eyes, he said. "Heck no, Lily, we know you wouldn't, er, couldn't do anything like that. Is there anything I can do for you, do you need a light bulb changed or something?" He looked almost hopeful.

Before I could answer, the three of us heard yelling from the above walkway, which bordered the marina. "Hurry up Lee, we are all waiting for you!" Then a mirage of giggles. Looking up, I could see three or four slim brunettes in jeans and jackets with golf clubs, smiling at Lee.

Looking quizzically at Lee, who was then a beet red, I replied, "I don't think you have time to change any light bulbs just now, but thanks for asking."

Lee didn't bother to answer, but dashed to the back of the boat to find his missing clubs and then sped off to join his bevy of brunette beauties.

"He's quite the guy, isn't he?" Smiled Captain Mike. "Light bulb. Now I've heard everything. Anyway,

Lily, don't worry, things will straighten out in no time." Touching his captain's hat brim, he turned and went down the galley steps out of view.

Well at least I have some island inhabitants' belief of my innocence. Though I'd rather have the police force's. I looked north toward where the Sea Mist was moored, but no life showed aboard the vessel. Peter must be sleeping or working on a project inside. I pondered going over to see him, but decided that he needed some time alone. We had been together most of the day yesterday and then in the evening. He probably needed a breather from me. Even though I certainly didn't from him.

I returned to the cabin to resume my Sunday routine. Casually sipped coffee, ate toasted bagels with cream cheese and read the paper. With a smile, I recalled Lee's earlier offer to change my light bulbs. Was that a new come-on line? Though he looked so innocent when he said it, with his baby blue eyes and cherubic face, I believed he was probably serious. A change of light bulb wasn't really what I needed just now, thanks all the same. My smile was soon squelched for I turned to the local section of the paper which was frothed with information concerning the demise of both Wardell's, though speculation was kept at a minimum - at least in print.

Another Death on Private Island

Hat Island has had its share of deaths recently. Four days ago the body of island resident, Sanford Wardell, 67, was found on the shore near Chalk Cliff. Initial consensus was made by authorities that Mr. Wardell fell to his death from Chalk Cliff, a 300 foot embankment that faces southeast toward Clinton on Whidbey Island. Final autopsy concluded, however, that Mr. Wardell died by blunt force trauma prior to the fall; authorities are still investigating. Yesterday, Mr. Wardell's wife,

> **Vivian, 65, was found dead in their island residence. The cause of death is pending toxicology and autopsy results, but preliminary findings point toward suicide. Ironically, the island has not had a death on its shores since 1873, when homesteader Peter Goutre was found murdered, reportedly for his rumored fortune. A killer was never found.**

Well, at least the paper did not mention any suspects, and especially not me. I stared at the article. What happened? It was almost as if a mysterious force had inhabited the island. Perhaps the ghost of Peter Goutre? Had he been lying low all these years and now decided to create havoc and seek revenge? With reluctance, I remembered my dream of the other night; it still gave me chills.

I stood up and tossed down the paper. Getting a bit irritated with my rambling thoughts and suppositions, I needed my Sunday walk. Calling Chuck from the back of the cabin, both of us headed out the door.

Cutting once again across the island toward the Gravel Bunker, my destination was the sandy beach. I could throw sticks for Chuck and contemplate my tumultuous life.

The beach was deserted, of course. I nestled down in the sand, curving my body into the minute particles. I had thrown a large stick for Chuck when we had reached the shore, and he now carried it around as if a prize. Reluctant to give it up, he finally lay down in the sand a few feet from me and began some earnest chewing.

Digging my feet into the sand, I leaned back against a log. Sand fleas jumped around my legs, evidently disturbed by my burrowing into their home. They are harmless enough, and would drill and carve new areas to explore away from my offending body.

I gazed out at the bay, facing southwest toward Whidbey Island. The Mukilteo-Clinton ferries were right on schedule, shuttling their passengers every 20 minutes to Mukilteo then Clinton and simultaneously passing each other in the middle of the channel each cruising the opposite direction. Since it was such a clear November day, the sun glinted off the ferry windows and made the surrounding waters appear as if glass. I felt the tension unwind from my body. The lapping water was soothing. *I felt like a drink.* Perhaps Detective Anton had been right. I may be drinking too much. I had been so enthralled with Peter that I immediately reached for the wine to calm my nerves as well as give me courage to pursue him. In addition, since the deaths of both Sanford and Vivian, I had drank to ease the distress I had felt. My stomach ached. I felt so alone, unloved and uncared for. Smitten as I was with Peter, I was unsure of his feelings. Leaving this morning so early, without a word, had somehow driven home my doubts in our relationship, if one at all. Was it the start of something between us? I thought about the evening before. Peter had made splendid love to me. Passionate kisses skimmed my body and he touched areas, which had never been caressed in such a manner before. I had ached for him. Remembering, I still did.

I was all of a sudden angry with myself. When had I become so wanton? Certainly not in my many years of marriage to Ben. I could have cared less. Was I now approaching the infamous sexual peak for women in their late thirties, or was I so starved for affection that I had thrown myself into a situation without second thought? Burying my face into my knees, I sat in the sand, contemplating a love affair when I should have been trying to help solve the murders of Sanford and maybe even Vivian Wardell. Deaths seemingly connected to me.

Chuck had evidently tired of his stick for he stuck his cold, wet nose into my neck. I put my arms about his damp, salty body and cried. Cried in sorrow for Sanford and Vivian, but most of all for the loss of myself and most importantly, my pride.

N. R. De Witte

Chapter Twenty-Six

Wind blew the trees above Chalk Cliff. I stood below and gazed at the magnificent sand crevices. Carved formations derived from weather and the occasional teen attempting to carve their latest heart-throb's initials into the sand bank. How easy it would be, if all one had to do was to carve initials into the sand...

Standing in the area where I had discovered Sanford Wardell's body, I wondered what had happened. Had Sanford had some enemy from his past that had tracked him to the island and disposed of him? My imagination was vivid, and I could conjure up several different scenarios, each with plausible, and some outlandish, reasons for his death. Unfortunately, the little sensible voice within mocked me, urging me to accept that the island may have a true killer lurking about. I thought about island possibilities. Remembering distinctly when Sanford and Ralph Waters had words regarding Ralph's operation of his four-wheeler. Sanford had been adamantly opposed to Ralph's speeding along the roadway in front of the Wardell house, pluming dust as he sped by. In fact, he had pitched such a fit at a community meeting one evening, that the board had banned all four-wheelers for a trial period of three months. After which time their use would be revisited and guidelines established for, and in consideration of, the harmony for all island residents. Ralph had been furious and had held Sanford in direct blame.

To kill him, over a four-wheeler? It was a pitiful motive and not one even worth repeating to Detective Anton, who would think I was trying to protect myself anyway.

I studied the yellow security-taped area. The police had picked up every stitch of litter, in hopes of securing a clue or bit of evidence. This portion of the beach was now the cleanest I had seen in many years. As in most cases of growing population, the more people, the more mess and unfortunately, that was true even on a small private island.

At the sounds of gulls, I turned and looked out toward Everett. The Scott Paper Mill was spewing smoke; the harbor was alive with vessels, most notably the naval fleet. Another pollutant for the bay, another swipe at sea life and life as we had known it. Progress once again.

Sighing, I called for Chuck and headed north, the marina my destination. The tide was coming in, and I hoped to make it back without having to wade. Though many a time I have removed my shoes, rolled up my pant legs and splashed through the salt brine, dodging drift and sliding over logs to make it home.

I climbed from the beach and cut behind a section of tiny cabins perched on the southwest tip of the island. I plowed through the tall marsh-like vegetation. The earth in this area was almost like desert sand, with tall reedy grasses covering a good amount of land, abutting bordering alder trees and eventually sloping into the island hills. The cabins that dotted this stretch of island had been here as long as I could remember and certainly before that! Most had been modified from the gray shacks of yesterday to charming bungalows. Though not as elaborate as the southwest side of the island, they were still comfortable enough with their large glossy windows, fireplaces to keep the chill off and television antennas for evening entertainment. Unlike the posh side of the island, hardly any residents lived in this area year round. One of the reasons was the bay and lack of transportation to the area other than by boat. Vessels were moored by buoy and even the best set-up could eventually break, sending a boat drifting off on the sound. Just a couple of years ago, an island resident had lost his 24 foot cruiser in the midst of a summer storm. It had broken loose from the mooring buoy and had drifted all the way to Port Susan Bay, several miles from its original location. Fortunately for the owner, the boat was found unharmed. Two other residents had been more fortunate as their boats had broken from their buoys, but had floated toward shore and had been trapped by the breakwater. Needless to say, storms can be exciting to watch as the rain crawls across the bay and lightening snaps bright light against the skies. But when there is a boat moored on a nearby buoy, apprehension and sleepless nights abound. Kind of like life.

The tide was coming in rapidly and I knew when I rounded the bend off Section I and passing the tiny row of 12 cabins, that I would indeed have to wade. I took off my shoes and tied the laces together, looping them around my neck. Rolling up my pant legs, I stepped into the salt water. It was freezing. Never really warm, November had indeed iced up the temperature even more. Teeth chattering, I waded toward the marina.

Chuck was barking, again, and I was reluctant to venture near enough to see what the problem was. One dead body in a lifetime was just fine with me - I'd be damned if I wanted to discover two - especially in a matter of days!

However, my fears were short-lived as curiosity got the better of me and I waded over next to a section of bulkhead that waves were slapping merrily. Chuck was seemingly hovering over something, and whining. Nudging him aside, I self-consciously peeked. There, in the brine and seaweed, perched on a piece of drift, sat a kitten. A tiny, drenched, and from all appearances, nearly a dead one. Gingerly, I picked the thing up. It was still warm, and I could feel its heart beating in the palm of my hand - albeit slowly. It was such a small thing, reasoning it couldn't be much more than five to six weeks of age. I glanced about, but could see nothing in the form of a mother cat. Somehow the poor dear had wandered off from Mom and got stranded by the incoming tide. There are wild cats on the island. Left behind by homeowners or guests, not intentionally of course, but because they become scared in their new environment and wander away, some never to return. Some survive the winter and some do not. During the summer months, vacationers take pity and feed them; however, winter months they are left to fend for themselves. The cats scavenge the beach for any meal they may find including dead fish and poultry bones.

There wasn't much I could do with this little kitten, but to take it along home with Chuck and me and try to save it. Carefully, I placed the small sodden bundle in my over-large slicker pocket, sure to leave the corner of the flap open for air. If it lived, I shall christen it "Lucky" - for it would need all the luck in world just now.

N. R. De Witte

Chapter Twenty-Seven

When I had reached the beach to the marina, I was able to sit down and replace my shoes as well as roll down my pant legs. Small comfort, as the pant legs were soaked through from the splashing I had incurred. Teeth chattering still, I rapidly ascended the trail to the marina anxious to get home to dry off and take care of my new little kitten still lodged unmoving in my slicker pocket.

As I walked past the marina, head bent down against the wind, I did glance toward the Sea Mist. Disappointment gnawed at me as I saw no sign of life. Perhaps Peter had taken the ferry back to town for additional supplies...perhaps he was trying to avoid me.....perhaps I thought too much.

Someone called out from behind me, somewhat muffled with the wind but I recognized the voice and clenched my teeth together in aggravation. Turning, I saw Detective Anton emerging from the tiny marina office heading toward me. Eyes gleaming, he didn't seem to miss a thing, taking in my disheveled appearance, sodden shoes and wet pant legs. I coldly studied him in return (literally), bundled up in his overcoat, hair blowing in the wind, though he didn't seem to notice or perhaps even care. When within a couple of feet of me he said, "Ms. Martin, so glad to see you. We need to have another little chat, I'm afraid."

"Well, detective, as you can see, I'm not in the best shape right now for a chat. I'm cold, wet, tired and hungry. And," I added with a touch of malice in my voice, "Need a drink. You will have to catch me later." I turned on my heel and started rapidly on my way, however, before I could get far, he was beside me, speaking low yet in a determined tone. "Sorry if you are in discomfort, but I have to speak to you, NOW!"

I did not stop walking, but continued my way home. Detective Anton doggedly followed me, dodging muddy pot holes as he went along. I relished the fact that his fancy dress shoes were now sporting mud encased soles. Both of us certainly had a stubborn streak.

Opening the cabin door, I shoved it back against him, but he was ready. Fending off the door, he entered the cabin and shut the door softly behind him. Chuck had snaked through both sets of our legs and now was on the rug in front of the fireplace and licking himself dry.

I headed toward the closet and removed an empty shoe box from the top shelf and grabbed a dish towel from the kitchen. Without removing my drenched slicker, I knelt next to Chuck by the fire, and carefully removed the sodden bundle of fur from my coat pocket. I heard a small intake of breath from behind me, and surmised that Detective Anton was watching every move I was making. Gingerly, I laid the kitten in the bedding and placed the shoe box close to the fire. The kitten was still breathing and its eyes had a slight slit look to them. Rolling back on my heels, I stood and removed my slicker, hanging it over the back of the breakfast bar chair.

"Excuse me, detective." I said tightly through still clenched teeth (I'd have TMJ if this kept up), "but I need to take a hot shower before I catch cold." Heading toward the back, I added snidely, "Make yourself at home."

I could feel his eyes boring into my retreating backside. What was so important that he needed to follow me home? Or, had he come to arrest me. Well, right now I just didn't care. I wanted a hot shower, something warm and dry to put on and a drink. In that order, and arrest or no arrest I was going to get it!

Chapter Twenty-Eight

The shower rejuvenated me. My thoughts cleared as the sprays of hot water littered my body and I could feel the tension ease from my limbs. Out of the shower, I towel-dried my hair and slipped into a thick terry robe. Shoving my feet into moccasins, I combed back my short hair, applied lipstick and a squirt of fragrance, though I didn't really know why…what did I care what I looked like or for that matter smelled like in front of Detective Anton?

When I returned to the kitchen, I found Detective Anton on bended knee in front of the kitten. He was making funny coddling sounds, but as he heard my approach, stiffened up and got to his feet. I did not like the way his eyes gleamed as he took in my appearance. But, in all honesty, he did have beautiful eyes. Again, I caught myself; good God, when had I started looking at Detective Anton's eyes? He annoyed me, with his secret smiles and superior air.

I watched him as he withdrew his ink pen from his jacket pocket. Hands, nice hands, perfectly sized and manicured. It is said that a man's hands….damn! Giving myself a mental shake I stalked over to the fridge and removed some opened wine left from the previous afternoon. At the Detective's uplifted brow, I mirthlessly smiled, lifted my newly poured wine glass and in a half-way salute announced, "Red wine, good for the heart. Here's to you!" I downed a good half of the glass, and then pronounced, just to disgust him, "Yum."

If the Detective disapproved, he didn't say, instead he commented, under his breath, "Ms. Martian, you are just on the edge of odd, and not a bit dull."

Purposely, I perked up, brightened (in what I hoped was a most annoying fashion) and replied, "Why thank you Detective, that's one of the nicest things I've heard in a long time."

Wanting the Detective to be on his merry way, I gave in and blurted out my suspicions regarding Ralph Waters. I never have been one to keep information to myself and with the aid of my wine, it was easier to let the information slip from my lips. I was disappointed at his reaction.

"That's it?" He looked at me aghast. "A four-wheeler?"

"Well, people get killed over the silliest things these days…" I trailed, slightly coloring.

"For your information, and I'm surprised you don't know this, Ralph Waters is away in Arizona for the holidays, unless he flew up to purposely do Sanford Wardell in." He smiled, almost devilishly.

I gave him the benefit of one of my distasteful looks, which didn't seem to phase him at all, swallowed a large gulp of wine and promptly choked. Sputtering and coughing I bent and tried to regain my composure, thus revealing a deep v-shape in the front of my robe. Detective Anton scurried across the floor to my side and promptly proceeded to bang me on the back.

"If you please," I managed to say, "I'm fine." I backed away from him. Visions of those handsome hands on my back did queer things to my insides. Disgusted, I made for the chair perched before the front room window and sat down, breathing deeply to compose myself.

The Detective watched me curiously. "Did you know that you are all red and splotchy?" He queried.

I glared at him, self-consciously clutching the front of my robe together, and replied heatedly, "From coughing. Must you be so observant?"

He did not reply. Instead, pulled a pair of red gloves, gold bells ensconced around each cuff, from his pocket and jingled them in front of me. "Have you seen these before?" He asked.

Stunned, I stared. Heart hammering, I said a bit too loudly, "My gloves. Where did you find them? I've looked everywhere!"

"So these ridiculous looking things are yours. Figures. They were found under the front seat of your jeep. The logical reason there were no prints other than your own." He held up a hand to silence me. "Please let me continue." Walking to the window and gazing out, he spoke low and softly, "No prints, but some hair fibers were found. Gray in the back where the shoe was. Most certainly Wardell's, but we are running forensics. Dark hair was retrieved from the front seat as well as blonde. Have you lent your vehicle to any one with dark hair?"

I didn't pay much attention as he had a beautiful voice. I sat and listened, quietly absorbing the tone and texture. It was sexy....

"Ms.   Martian!   Are   you listening?"

Mortified   at   my   jumbled thoughts and being roused by the Detective, I jumped up suddenly and exclaimed, "No one drives my jeep but me and maybe my sons, but they have   been   gone   for   over   three months. Both boys are blonde any way. I need to get dressed." With that feeble remark, I high-tailed it down the hall and into my bathroom.

I   splashed   cold   water   in   my face and stared at my reflection. My green eyes were enormous and had a haunted look. My face was flaming - I   was   indeed   going   off   my   rocker thinking   those   kinds   of   *thoughts* about   Detective   Anton.   I   dressed quickly   in   a   pair   of   jeans   and   a sweatshirt,   donned   my   slippers   once again and *did not look* back into the mirror,   but   headed   back   to   the kitchen.

The   moment   I   stepped   out   into the   hall,   I   smelled   cooking.   I inwardly fumed. How dare he presume to   peruse   my   kitchen,   let   alone touch my belongings. But, there he was, sport coat off, sleeves rolled up (revealing hairy, sexy arms) and busily chopping a shriveled tomato and wilted green onion.

He did not look at me, but murmured over his shoulder, "You need to eat. So far, each time I've seen you, you've done nothing but drink. I've looked into your cupboards. You have hardly anything there, besides soup, worth consuming. No wonder you are so thin."

My mouth dropped, and I gaped at him. How dare he. How dare he barge into my home, muddle up my thoughts, insinuate I drink too much and to top it off, claim the I don't eat well and am too thin. Well, too bad. I'm nothing to him, and certainly none of his business. I glared at his back, though it didn't seem to bother him. Unlike women, he evidently did not have a sixth sense nor eyes in the back of his head. Too bad, my withering look would have done him in. I then enjoyed sticking my tongue out at him. Unfortunately, he turned and looked at me just about then.

Ignoring my childish behavior, the Detective plopped down a plate holding a delicious looking omelet on the breakfast bar, complete with buttered wheat toast. He motioned me over with a hook of his hand. Well, I fumed as I made my way over to a seat, it certainly did not take him long to find his way around my kitchen. Must be the detective in him.

I pondered not eating for about a split second, but my stomach was growling and the heavenly scent of the omelet was overwhelming. Giving in, I took a bite. Divine, it was all I could do not to swoon. My, but the detective was a surprise. A man that could cook was rare in my book. My ex's specialty was ordering out pizza or heating a can of chili.

"Ms. Martian, are you with me? You must be, your food is almost gone. Perhaps you've just been concentrating on my great culinary ability." He smiled.

Giving him the benefit of one of my scornful looks, I replied, "You are entirely too modest, detective."

Arms crossed and leaning against the kitchen counter, adjacent to where I was perched, he grinned wider as if pleased by my snide comment.

I was just about finished with my meal when he stuck a glass of milk in front of me and commented, "A woman your age needs calcium. Osteoporosis, you know."

Somehow that did it. He had succeeded in not only implying that I was a scrawny woman with a taste for booze, but had topped it off with the greatest insult of all - *age*. He implied that *I was old*. That was hitting way below the belt.

I did not drink the milk, but slammed down my fork instead, jumped from the bar stool and glared at him as I turned to walk into the living room.

Steaming mad, I bent down by the kitten and gently touched it to take sure it was still alive. Warmth and pulsation greeted me along with a feeble "Mew." My momentary anger at the detective was forgotten as I was suddenly elated that the kitten was possibly going to live.

Detective Anton bent down next to me, and with his index finger gently caressed the top of the kitten's head. He said, softly, "Ms. Martian, did I say or do something to offend you?"

Without looking at him, but watching him stroke the kitten's head, I replied, "Oh no, Detective. What could have given you that idea?" I know I sounded sharp and bitter. The cad, he just chuckled.

He got up and went back to the kitchen where I heard dinner dishes clatter, utensils chime and water filling in the sink. I continued to fume, but it did not do much good as he seemed fairly good at ignoring me. Giving up, I got up and returned for my half empty glass of wine that I had left on the breakfast bar.

While the detective did the dishes and tidied the kitchen, a fact that I did reluctantly enjoy, I studied him from under my lashes. He was a capable man. Deftly he washed, rinsed and stacked the dishes. Wiped the counter top and even straightened the dish towel and rag. He seemed very comfortable in the kitchen and I concluded that he most likely lived alone. Not that a married man would not be able to perform such functions, but from my own experiences with the opposite sex, just highly unlikely.

The detective switched off the kitchen light and headed into the living room to join me, rolling down the sleeves of his blue chambray shirt as he entered the room. I did not look at him, but could feel my face growing warm. I honestly did not know why.

Detective Anton perched on the edge of the worn sofa and leaned toward me. I had finally gotten brave enough to look at him. "Ms. Martian, in regards to Vivian Wardell the autopsy is not conclusive yet, but I'm hedging my bets that it wasn't an overdose. Hence, not a suicide." At my forlorn look, he held up his hand and continued, "We should have the rest of the tests back by tomorrow and then know what we are dealing with."

"Why are you telling me this? Isn't this information supposed to be a police secret or something? What if I invent some story to protect myself." I whispered the last part of the sentence.

"I want you to be careful. Something is out of whack on the island, and you need to be wary." At my surprised look, he went on to say, "I really don't believe you have had anything to do with the deaths, but someone may be trying to incriminate you, or perhaps you are just unlucky; being in the wrong place at the wrong time. At any rate, you need to be cautious. Just on the safe side, I'm leaving one of the officers here on the island for the time being. The groundskeeper said he would put him up. It may deter further things from happening, though I think there will be no more incidents. Both Sanford and Vivian Wardell may have been premeditated targets, who knows." He stood up then and walked over to his coat which was flung on the back of the sofa. I could only stare at him. I don't know what I really was feeling, possibly a mix of relief, fright and again, searing confusion.

Detective Anton did not smile at me as he put on his coat, just looked at me curiously. I stared back and our eyes locked for a brief second. He then said, "Lock the door behind me." Turned and left.

I got up and locked the door behind him as ordered and leaned back against it trying to gather my scattering thoughts. Finally, pushing away from the door, I crossed over to the radio, flipped it on and returned to my chair by the fire.

Various "oldies" spewed throughout my small cabin while I sat in my chair as if mesmerized. Tons of emotions coursed through my body. I sipped my wine and reflected. How very strange life was. Just when you think you have it all figured out and relatively at peace, something springs up to disturb the balance, changing the pace and making unsettling demands. My life had been topsy-turvy since late last week, and was progressing rapidly on a collision course to where I didn't even begin to grasp. And, as I sat and pondered what was

happening, I had to come to grips
with what was upsetting me the most
- the deaths of the Wardells, my
apparent one-night stand with Peter,
or my growing attraction to
Detective Anton?

Chapter Twenty-Eight

Since it was the end of the weekend, and Monday would be a notorious transcription day, I decided to go to bed early. Besides, Peter had not stopped by to see me, though I hadn't been surprised. Perhaps I had enough surprises with Detective Anton's visit. Whether Peter was fighting demons of his own, or knew that the Detective had been at my place, I didn't know. I did realize, however, that Peter did not like conflict nor did he want to become involved, either with me, or apparently my current troubles.

Turning down the fireplace damper, I checked on my newest

233

addition to the family. Lucky was sleeping soundly and I felt encouraged. With Chuck padding behind me, I turned off the lights in the kitchen and headed toward my bedroom. Glancing out the bedroom window through the sheers, I could see the moon, which was full and brightly shining. I hoped that the full moon would not bring out anymore ghouls this evening, I didn't think I would survive it. As I crawled beneath the covers, I caught myself humming a Dusty Springfield tune I heard earlier on the radio, *"You don't have to say you love me, just be close at hand, you don't have to stay forever, I will understand, believe me, believe me, believe me..."* my eyes filled with tears and my thoughts exploded in several different directions. Peter, the murders, and most uncomfortably, Detective Anton with his sexy voice and beautiful hands. I turned onto my side and forced myself to sleep.

I awoke to the sound of the phone. I hadn't remembered to turn down the volume and to cease the shrill ringing, leapt from bed and scooted into the kitchen to end the din.

"Hello." I said, breathlessly.

"Well, thanks for returning my call." Gert was certainly peeved as I could feel her anger emanating through the phone. Belatedly, I remembered her frenzied call of Saturday night, and summons to return her call as soon as possible, which I had not done.

"Remember me? Or are you up to your eye balls with a man? No time for old friends?" She was certainly in rare form this early in the morning, as glancing at the nearly wall clock, determined it to be shortly after 7:00 AM.

"Sorry, Gert. I should have called you, but Saturday was a day from hell. They found Vivian Wardell, dead. The Detective pounced on me the minute I got home from the mainland. I guess I haven't had a breather since. My thoughts have really been in a pickle." I apologized, sighing deeply as I explained.

From her tone, I knew that Gert had simmered down, most likely in sympathy for me. "Damn. I know about the lady. That's why I called you. Doc had done some interesting tests. The Mrs. was full of insulin. Interesting, huh. And, no anti-depressant medication either." I heard the smugness in her voice, guessing for some reason that she was certainly satisfied with herself. I hoped she was being careful, not calling so anyone could hear, conflict of interest, etc. Gert may be a dynamo at her job, but in the hands of corporate protocol, was playing with fire letting these little snippets of information privy to an outsider, and a murder suspect as well.

"So she was full of insulin. You and I know that anyone in advanced age increases their insulin productivity tremendously. That's not such a big deal." I reasoned with her. Still reluctant to accept the fact that someone did Vivian Wardell in.

Gert explained slowly and pronouncing each word clear and concise, as if I were a child or a dunce. "No...that's not such a big deal. But a tiny, well-hidden injection site is." If I hadn't been so shocked at her comment, I would have noted again the obvious satisfaction in her voice. She was having the time of her life.

"What do you mean, well-hidden injection site?" I exclaimed, now fully awake and beginning to chill.

"Doc ran those infra-red lights over the body. You know, those new lights he's so fond of. Well, everything looked as it should. But he got up to the head. I am proud to say I work for that man, for he is good. A little strange at times, all those dead bodies and all, but he is good - I'll give him that." she rattled on.

"Gert, hurry up. Tell me what happened!" I intervened, trying to spur her along to tell me what was found rather than accounting the fine attributes of the coroner.

"Okay, okay. Now this is sneaky. There was an injection, a fraction of an inch away from her left ear lobe. Doc wouldn't have found it, but the way the body was turned and her hair all mussed up, it almost leapt out at him. He magnetized the area and sure enough, an injection site. Can't say that she was trying to double pierce her ears now, can we?" Gert chuckled at her own humor. I did not find anything funny, as I was far too stunned.

"Are you with me kiddo? Hey, say something!" Gert commanded, a worried note to her voice.

Meekly, I replied. "I'm okay. Just surprised, confused and all of sudden not feeling too well. I'm going to go now, Gert. But I promise I'll give you a call real soon. Thanks for the info." With that, I hung up. Hand over mouth I succeeded to make it to the bathroom before any gags took affect. That was a definite problem with me, stress and unsettling circumstances tended to upset my stomach and this time I was hit ten-fold.

I sat back on the bathroom floor, eyes watering and trying to absorb what Gert had just told me. My mind was active with island resident maladies. Yet I could not pinpoint anyone that I knew of as incurring a bad enough case of diabetes mellitus to warrant insulin therapy. *Except Matt*, my subconscious acknowledged. But Matt wouldn't harm a fly, he wasn't even a consideration. My thoughts moved elsewhere.

Bob and Betty Brummelman were off and on again in poor health. I knew from medical history that Bob was watching his diet due to age-induced diabetes. But according to records (I transcribed for his doctor), he was not yet insulin dependent. Part of me wished that he was, the way he and Betty had snubbed me Sunday afternoon as they had driven past on their way home from the mainland and ferry trip. Bob pretended to focus on the road, but I could see through the windshield that Betty was saying something to him and avoiding my direction. It was clear to me that they thought I had something to do with the Wardell's deaths. Well, the shoe's on the other foot, so to speak, perhaps they were the guilty party. I bet Detective Anton would be interested in my deduction. Unfortunately, however, I could not tell the Detective unless I revealed my source, which would open up a whole other can of worms. Besides, I was not feeling up to sparring with the Detective at the moment, and needed to get my feelings for him squared away lest they show all over my face the next time I saw him.

My rumination was brought up short by a soft mewing sound. I had forgotten about the kitten! Quickly, I shuffled over to the shoebox, bent and peered inside. Wide blue eyes stared back at me, and a small pink tongue flicked out of a tiny mouth. Perhaps she was still weak, but she certainly did not seem to be afraid of me. I carefully picked up the fluffy bundle and took it into the kitchen. Placing her on the floor I reached into the fridge for my milk. With a full saucer in front of her, she shyly edged to the rim and as instinct took over, rapidly began to lap the milk. I smiled watching her and felt like a proud mother whose baby had learned to walk. I pulled the kitten away from the milk after a few minutes, as I didn't want her getting sick. No telling how long she had been without nourishment. Gently placing her back into the shoebox, I watched as she nodded back to sleep, evidently the effort given to ingesting the milk had worn her out.

Having showered quickly, donned jeans and sweater and brewed coffee, I checked the modem to see if the transcription had downloaded, which it had. I was glad to have work to do to help occupy my thoughts other than the constant thoughts about the Wardell's, Peter and the Detective.

Three hours later, I wasn't so sure. My head ached and my shoulder had a kink in it from too much sitting and tense typing. And I had failed at trying to avoid thoughts of the current crisis of my life.

While getting up to stretch, I traveled into the living room to gaze out the window. My kitten still slept in her shoebox, and I knew that eventually she would mend, gain strength and most likely be a holy terror. I wouldn't have it any other way.

Gulls hovered over the bay as the tide was out and temptations of beached fish, bait or clams inviting. The gulls destiny of food encouraged me to explore my lunch possibilities as well. Though I hadn't had much of an appetite of late, Detective Anton's opinion of my body spurred me toward lunch with a vengeance.

I heated some tomato soup, made toast and tea. And, for the benefit of caloric intake, liberally slathered butter on my toast and extra sugar was stirred into my tea. Scrawny indeed, I'd show that detective!

However, lunch can only last so long and I needed to get back to work. Replacing headphones and switching on the dictaphone, I once gain began pounding the keyboard. Sometimes transcription can be boring and I put myself on automatic pilot. Today, however, it was deja vu or something else para-normal because three of the cases I transcribed involved diabetes and treatment. Especially interesting were the signs and symptoms, anything I could use in pointing a finger at a shifty island resident. Unfortunately, besides the usual caution of diet, exercise and prompt medication intervals, nothing striking was divulged to help me in my investigation. Dejected, I finished the rest of the minutes in record time, and set the modem to download back to the mainland by 6 PM.

Dinner and the long hours to follow loomed ahead of me. Only past four, I was antsy and in need of something to do. However, I was not going to walk by the marina in case I ran into Peter. He may think I was purposely looking for him. Let him seek me out. I would be strong. Reaching into the cupboard, I grabbed a newly seasoned bottle of cabernet. Six years I had waited for this particular wine, and though I had no one special to share it with, decided that why not have it myself…wasn't I special? So, without much aplomb, I uncorked, poured, sniffed and swirled the burgundy liquid in one of my favorite cut-glass wine flutes. Admiring the color, I wandered into the living area to once again enjoy the view before darkness dimmed the daylight.

N. R. De Witte

Chapter Twenty-Nine

I spent the evening reading and actually relaxing for the first time in days. Leisurely I sipped my wine thoroughly engrossed in a new mystery novel.

A bit after 8:00 PM, Chuck lifted his head and pricked his ears. I watched him curiously, as I did not expect visitors. However, I wasn't ruling out the possibility of Detective Anton popping back up or perhaps even a visit from Peter. A knock on the door and the deep voice of Peter confirmed my visitor. I hurried to the door to let him in.

Peter scurried past me and made for the warmth of the fire. I closed the door and tried not to be miffed that I hadn't heard from him in the last day or so. Settled back in my chair, I watched him warm his hands. Eventually Peter turned and gave me a lop-sided grin. Thoughts of his indifference toward me and doubts about our relationship seemed to trickle aside. I was hit anew by his handsomeness and sexuality. I smiled back.

"Glad to see you, Lily. Been working long and hard on the schooner. Sorry I haven't been to see you before now. Time just got away from me." He seemed so genuine.

"Oh, that's okay, Peter. I've been busy as well (yeah, sure, drinking, listening to sad music and visiting with Detective Anton regarding a murder suspect skulking the island, my little inner voice mocked me.) I smiled at Peter as he approached and stood up to receive his embrace. Kissing me on the side of my neck, the tender spot just below my ear lobe…..longing stirred inside.

Peter broke away long enough to utter, "God, you are so beautiful!" before bending down to capture my lips with his. Passion took us away, and it was many moments before I could carefully break away to catch my breath.

He watched me as I crossed to the kitchen to get the wine, an extra glass and some crackers and cheese. Bringing our treats into the living room, we sat together in front of the fire absorbing the warmth, each other and the fine wine.

Much later, as Peter prepared to leave, we made plans to meet for lunch the next day aboard the schooner.

"Perhaps we could venture to Everett again, if everything seems ship shape with the boat." He suggested.

"Okay by me. Sounds like fun." I replied. To heck with Detective Anton and his order about not leaving the island, I was delighted that I could be with Peter again and no pompous detective was going to stop me!

I slept well that evening, doubts no longer lingered in my mind and even clouds of Sanford and Vivian Wardell did not enter my dreams. However, when I awoke the next morning, I had a dull ache behind my eyes and vague memories of Peter Goutre and blasts of gunshots during the night.

Since Monday was the usual classic hectic day at the clinic, I wasn't too surprised at the bulk of work that had downloaded during the night. Determined to keep my lunch date with Peter, I began transcribing at 6:00 AM and fortified myself with coffee and toasted bagel.

Most of the transcription was easy and I was optimistic that working until noon I would be at a good stopping point and could tackle the rest when I returned.

"Patient has carpal tunnel syndrome bilaterally, worse in the right, left probably not a surgical candidate but the right definitely is. She will be scheduled at her convenience after the holidays." The holidays, it was now Tuesday and Thursday was Thanksgiving. Peter would most likely be gone within the next two days and I was scheduled to be at Gert's for the Thanksgiving festivities. This year, however, I didn't feel so festive, owing the feeling to missing my boys, the island unrest and Peter's pending departure.

I was just typing up the last 30 minutes of transcription, "Her incision is healed, and sutures and splint are removed. Patient can start working on ROM exercises and return to normal activities and work by November 28," when the phone rang as I put the finishing touches on the last sentence. Relieved, I saved the disk, turned off the computer and got up to answer it.

"Ms. Martian," Detective Anton's voice echoed from the receiver. I immediately tensed and could feel butterflies in my stomach. My face infused with warmth. I replied, "Why, hello Detective. I'm just on my way out and can't talk to you just now."

"On your way out? Hopefully not off the island, as you are aware, I told you to stay put." He seemed to enunciate each word carefully. Like I was a dimwit or something.

"Stay put? But you said that I wasn't a suspect. You said you believed me!" I could hear my voice becoming higher and higher in pitch.

"Murder suspect not to me mind you, but in the eyes of the department and the law, you still have things to explain. Therefore, I urge you to remain on the island. If something comes up and it is important that you leave, let me know. You have my card and number." He clicked off and I could tell by his tone of voice that he was annoyed with me as if dealing with a recalcitrant child.

I was furious, and certainly did not plan to sit around on the island when I could be off sailing with Peter. One aspect of my personality is that if someone tells me no, then I'm more apt to go ahead and do it just for spite. And that was the case in this instance. I was going with Peter and what Detective Anton didn't know wouldn't hurt him, or me. *How wrong I was.*

N. R. De Witte

Chapter Thirty

Anxious to look my best for Peter, even though we would be in the gusty wind maneuvering the sailboat, I was careful to dress warmly in flattering lupine blue to accentuate my blond hair. In addition, I applied just enough makeup to liven-up my good points. After dabbing on a hopefully seductive fragrance, I hurried off to lock Chuck in the shed and to meet Peter at the marina.

Peter was rolling up the mooring lines having already secured the sails. Evidently he decided to sail to Everett after all and we'd most likely lunch on board or even at the Port of Everett again. I was excited at the thought, and near giddy when I reached his side. He smiled as I neared, and gave me a quick peck on the cheek and said, "Go on aboard Lily, and get comfortable. I would prefer you sit below until I get this thing out of the marina. I'll be running all over and don't want to run you down."

I smiled, and gave a mock salute, "Aye, aye, Captain!" and commenced down the aft steps to the galley below.

As Peter sailed out of the marina harbor, I sat at the galley table. Sitting there, I noticed a copy of Chapman Pelting, Seamanship and Small Boat Handling book in the case behind the seat along with some other books and magazines on various sailing topics. I picked up the heavy volume and began to thumb through it. The book was impressive and though first published in 1917, was still a mainstay with sea men young and old. Several articles were outlined in red. Though they meant nothing to me, Peter evidently had been studying the book in earnest being the novice sailor he was. As I casually leafed through the book something fluttered to the galley floor. Bending I picked up a picture of Peter with his arms about a very pretty brunette.

"Okay, Lil', come on up now. Coast is clear." Peter invited.

I climbed up the galley steps wondering about the woman in the picture with Peter. However, warmth was my major concern as upon entering the aft deck the wind immediately blew my hair in disarray and the chill bit into my bones. Tears welled in my eyes because of the elements. Heck, there goes the eye makeup! I dabbed at my eyes with a tissue just as Peter enfolded me in a hug and placed me in front of him as he steered the sloop's wheel. Well, I reasoned, I'm here with Peter now so she couldn't be that important!

Cozy and warmer, I could see that we were rapidly being ushered by the wind toward Everett. Though it was not raining, dark clouds seemed ominous above and I wasn't at all sure we would survive our trial run without a bit of dampness.

"How does she seem, Peter." I yelled up at him through the wind. Though by the smile on his face, I knew that so far he was pleased by the way things were going.

"Fine, just fine. I believe I fixed everything. She seems to be handling well. With this wind, it's a good test to put her through before I head up north."

I pasted a phony smile on my face, as I was extremely disappointed at his comment. I knew, of course, that it was only a matter of time before he had repaired the vessel and was on his way, but I was hoping for a bit more time.

What for I questioned myself, what did I expect from him? A pledge of undying love when we had just met days before?

Peter must have read my mind because he squeezed me tighter and said into my ear, "Sorry, Lily. But you knew I would have to leave. Let's forget about if for now and just have a fun day together. He tried to console me, but knew it would most likely not be too successful.

We made it to the Port of Everett without any mishaps. Peter was definitely pleased with the repairs and the schooner. We docked in the visitor's section, tied up lines, and situated sails. Disembarking, we ended up once again in Anthony's restaurant, but this time sat in the bar.

Sitting across from each other cradling glasses of Merlot, we were silent and the atmosphere a bit strained. Each of us evidently absorbed in our own thoughts. Peter's about his impending trip and mine about life without him or without anyone like him in my near future. Just when I had decided to experience life again, my chance at a relationship swiftly snatched away. I felt jilted.

When the waitress refilled our glasses of wine, we half-heartedly toasted, "To the Sea Mist." Though my heart wasn't in it; I wondered if his was.

The silence grew more and more uncomfortable and we both drank quickly, eager to get back to the schooner and head back toward the island, an easy escape from discussions of the heart, or lack of.

The wind was still strong, and unfortunately the looming clouds of earlier unloaded their burgeoning load. Rain pelted down upon us and thus accentuated the wind chill. It did not take much for Peter to urge me below. Not only did I want to keep dry, but did not relish the close proximity to him knowing that soon he would be far from my reach.

Between the wind and rain, the bay became rougher than before. Waves turned wild and the sloop listed to one side and then the next, time and again. Though I was confident of Peter's sailing ability, I was still somewhat nervous and anxious. I knew Peter had purchased some wine earlier, so I decided to scout around for a bottle, just to ease my nerves. Rummaging through his cabinets, I found what I did not expect. In the lower bottom drawer of the galley cabinet, a safe bet for stashing bottles I assumed, were several packets of syringes used by diabetics as the packaging displayed the "so fine, you could hardly feel it" logo. I was shocked. Visions of Peter feeling poorly and racing off to the pharmacy three days prior raced through my mind. But that was not all. Visions of Vivian Wardell popped in as well. Vivian with an injection site in her left earlobe, and excessive insulin in her body.

So stunned and intent on my discovery, I did not see Peter peeking through the galley door. He must have been checking up on me to see if the tumultuous ride had gotten the better of me. Unfortunately, it wasn't the ride but my discovery that had bested me.

"Lily, are you all right? What are you doing down there?" Peter exclaimed, trying to shove the hair and sea spray from his face as peered into the galley depths. Perhaps he didn't see me by the drawer I reasoned. Slowly I eased it back in place, but not before noticing the edge of a golden gilt frame, far too similar to the one perched on the oak mantel of Sanford and Vivian Wardell's home.

Peter evidently hadn't been suspicious of me, as he did not descend to the galley but returned to guiding the sloop back to the marina. I was vastly relieved when we entered the little harbor. My friends were there, and I would be safe. Peter wouldn't dare try anything in the midst of this populated copse. Populated my foot, I realized with a sinking heart, as gazing out the porthole I saw no one about. My imagination began to run away with me. Peter quickly killing me and stuffing my body in the sloop until he could safely leave the island and dispose of me in the murky green depths of Puget Sound. No one would be the wiser, as no one saw me leave and Detective Anton had forbade me to leave the island. What a fool I was. Blind infatuation and lust had prevented me from seeing the obvious. Peter, a perfect stranger, and diabetic no less, present at my house situated next to the Wardell's and now both of them dead. It all seemed to fit the puzzle so easily. Why was I so dumb?

"Lily, what are you doing? You looked spooked." Peter spoke carefully and somewhat warily as he climbed down the galley steps.

I stammered, backing away from him toward the bow. "Er, nothing. I'm doing nothing. Just don't feel too well. Gotta go." I tried to maneuver past him, but he blocked my way.

"I saw you in the drawer, and know what you found. You should have asked if you were looking for something in particular. I kind of have a problem with people going through my stuff." He spoke tightly.

"Um, sorry Peter. I didn't mean to be snooping, just looking for some wine to calm my nerves. But, I really have to go now." My eyes darted from side to side, trying to determine how best to get out of the boat, however, it was no good, I was pinned.

"Not so fast." Peter pulled me against him. His eyes were black and beady, no longer the gorgeous hazel of earlier. His once soft and tempting body did not mold to me as

261

it once had, but was firm and hard, no warmth emanating from its depths. I was scared. No, petrified. I felt my life passing before me in a wave of slow motion. Despair clawed at my gut as I realized I might never see or hold my sons again.

Strangely, as all of the emotions passed my face, Peter bent down and kissed me on the lips, stepped back and let me go. I slumped and stared into his eyes. They had returned to their normal color and he seemed to have a sad look upon his face. I turned then, and clamored up the galley steps, plummeted over the side of the schooner and dashed down the dock and up the ramp. Quickly looking into the marina office, I could not find Matt. No one was about. I looked over my shoulder, but could only see Peter pulling away from the dock. Shocked and relieved, I raced toward home to call Detective Anton.

Chapter Thirty-One

My hands were unsteady as I unlocked the cabin door. I banged my knee against the doorjamb as I hurried through and gingerly made my way to the phone, cursing under my breath. My heart was hammering as I searched the counter for the Detective's business card. Finally locating it under my pile of mail, I grabbed the phone and dialed.

The clerk that answered the Sheriff's office informed me that Detective Anton was not in. "But I have to speak to him, it's a matter of life and death!" I proclaimed loudly.

"Just a minute Miss, I'll pass you to Sergeant Reed." She seemed to be not that concerned…as if everyday she queried a caller's intent and placated appropriately.

"This is Sergeant Reed, how may I help you?" Visions of the freckled faced, red-haired youthful officer danced in my mind. Nevertheless, I introduced myself and stated my need to get in touch with the Detective.

"Well, you should be seeing him shortly Miss Martian, he is on the Island investigating. If he hasn't stopped by yet, you may want to try the crime scene where Mr. Wardell was found. The Detective wanted to take another look around. Should I let him know you are looking for him in case he calls? Is there anything I can do?" He seemed concerned, most likely because of my quivering voice.

I probably should have told him about Peter, but wanted for some reason to just tell the Detective and have him deal with it. I thanked the Sergeant, asked him to let Detective Anton know I wanted to

speak with him should he call, and
rung off.

Glancing out the front window,
I could see the tide was out far
enough for me to walk the beach over
to Section H and below to Chalk
Cliff. Perhaps I'd intercept the
Detective and be able to tell him my
suspicions about Peter.

I raced out the door, freed
Chuck from the shed and dashed down
the road toward the Gravel Bunker.
The rain pelted me, but my
adrenaline level was so high I could
not decipher the cold. Chuck ran
gleefully beside me, intrigued with
his master's unusual burst of energy
and enthusiasm. I got a stitch in my
side from running, and could feel
mascara smearing under my eyes. I
would look a real sight when I met
the Detective. Probably would scare
him. Would serve him right for
stirring up all those odd feelings
in me.

Passing the bunker, and row of
homes in Section H, I got to the
murder scene in short time,
laboriously breathing and clutching
my side from the run. Someone was

there all right, but it wasn't Detective Anton. The person bent over and digging behind the log where once Sandord Wardell's body had been was not an officer of the law. Hearing me behind him and with Chuck lapping at his face, he stood up and turned. I was shocked to see Dr. Sorenson.

I stared at him, and finally found words. "Dr. Sorenson, what are you doing here?" I was wary, for I didn't know what was going on. "I'm looking for Detective Anton. Have you seen him?" I inquired, trying to keep my curious gaze from the hole he had scratched in the sand by his feet.

Chuck, however, was less than discreet. Circling the doctor, he pawed at the ground and picked up something in his mouth. Like with all his treasures, he dashed off to leisurely explore and inspect his newly found prize.

Dr. Sorenson had been watching Chuck as well and yelled as the dog scampered away. "Bring that back! Hey mutt, did you hear me?"

The doctor turned to me, and said coldly. "Lily, have that dog get back here. He has something of mine. I must have just dropped it."

Incredulously I looked at him. "But doctor, I didn't see you drop anything, you were digging through the sand just now."

"That's right, I dropped it and was trying to find it. Now, if you please, get that dog back here." He virtually hissed at me. What was the problem with the good doctor? Usually so personable and calm, he was wired and sweating profusely. Perspiration beaded his brow and the underarms of his windbreaker were stained. Not wishing to rile him further, I called for Chuck. My dog trotted up to me, object of interest still clenched in his mouth. I tried prying apart his jaw, but before I knew it, Dr. Sorenson was at my side and beginning to inject something into Chuck's thigh while grabbing at his snout simultaneously. "What are you doing?" I cried, shoving his hand away and dislodging the needle before it had pierced any of my pet's flesh. Dr. Sorenson pushed me aside, but not before Chuck dropped the treasure from his mouth and scurried off toward some trees near Chalk Cliff.

I could only stare at the doctor. Clutching a syringe in one hand and retrieving a watch in the other, he almost was berserk. No, I reasoned, he was insane. Cautiously, I asked. "Why would you inject Chuck to get a watch, Doctor?" But the way he was looking at me, eyes no longer friendly but wild, strained and menacing, I knew. Without a doubt I knew. It wasn't Peter who had injected Vivian Wardell with insulin. It had been Dr. Sorenson. It wasn't Peter that had taken the pills in order to implicate suicide either, but Dr. Sorenson when he had reported back to the residence of the deceased. And, it had been Dr. Sorenson who had disposed of Sanford Wardell. I just knew it. He was one of the few people who knew where my car keys were hidden and who knew how to get to Chalk Cliff. As if reading my mind, Dr. Sorenson smiled. It was a wily smile, and terrifying. He then said in a strange, sing-song voice. "So, you have figured it out, have you? Always knew you were a smart woman, perhaps too smart for your own good." Then in a calmer, more normal voice he continued. "It was an accident, you know. I just wanted to know where my money had gone. The wind was wild and we were standing in his yard talking when a large branch blew down and hit him in the head. He died instantly. I panicked, borrowed your rig and threw him off Chalk Cliff." He then got louder and began sweating heavily again. "Vivian knew too much. But that doesn't matter now does it?"

I didn't like that comment. But was so scared and a little dimwitted that I could not think of a smart reply, only how to get out of this mess. Though the doctor was in his sixties, he was in superb shape. Avid jogger, his lean, strong body could out run me and with his bare hands no doubt snap my neck in two in nothing flat.

I backed up, preparing to turn and run anyway, but tripped over a piece of drift. Scampering backward, I watched as the doctor reached behind him for his bag and withdrew a vial of insulin. My eyes were glued to him and I could not force myself to stand, let alone run and escape. I watched as if in a slow motion movie, as he filled the syringe, squirt liquid from the tip and drop the vial back into the bag. He then turned toward me, advancing with the syringe clasped tightly in his hand.

Why couldn't I move? I just sat there in the sand watching him near me and so terrified that no sound would come out of my mouth. So similar to my dream of a few days earlier, which now seemed to be a premonition of some kind. Just as the doctor reached for my arm, another nightmare similarity occurred. Wavering just to the right of the doctor was a man, the man I had seen in my dream. The man with steely eyes of hatred and whose face slowly began dissolving to a mass of ghoulish flesh and membrane. I thought at first that I was hallucinating, but then Doctor Sorenson abruptly stopped what he was about to do looking up and over my head, and said with a quivering voice. "Who are you? What are you? Oh my God, No!"

Just as he uttered those words a shot rang out. Dr. Sorenson flew backward from the impact. He landed at an angle, propped against the uprooted tree where Sanford Wardell's body had been found. Evidently the shot had killed him instantly because he resembled a slouched rag-doll, blood seeping from his mouth, eyes staring and vacant.

I looked around to see if my ghoul was still about but could see no one, no one except Detective Anton standing on the edge of Section H's rock bulkhead arm still poised holding his service revolver.

I lay down in the sand and cried.

N. R. De Witte

Chapter Thirty-Two

It was no surprise that I wound up at Dan Compton's place again. Our interlude between island death's was becoming a habit, as was the brandy he stuffed into my hand as the Detective escorted me through the door.

Depositing me on the couch, Detective Anton removed my shoes, soaked coat, and covered me with a quilt. He had removed the brandy while removing my damp items and now shoved it back into my hands, ordering me to drink. "I can't believe I'm urging you to drink." Was all he said as he stood and headed out the door.

Dan and I sat once again in silence. We could hear the arrival of the helicopter as it made its way to the golf course green for landing. Poor Matt, he would be in another tizzy with the new onslaught of officers and inevitable reporters to come, not to mention the chewed-up green from the helicopter. I could just imagine him grousing about while Lee Treasure ate up the limelight and offered special golf deals to all the visitors. That would incite Matt even more. I was glad to be missing that certainty.

Detective Anton finally returned and announced that it was time to return to my place. He had apparently procured some medication from the Coroner and ordered me to take two of the small white caplets. "It will keep you calm and help you sleep." He quietly intoned. Not wishing to rile him or argue for that matter, I swallowed the pills.

Matt's face was gray. Whether from fatigue, or an already row with Lee, I didn't know. I was only glad to see him and from the wide smile he gave me, he was glad to see me as well. With Chuck at my side, we climbed into the bus. He drove cautiously up the hill to my cabin and assisted me through the door and situated me on the couch. Covering me with a quilt, he then stoked up the stove to warm up the room. However, no amount of wood would be able to dispel the chill I felt inside.

The pills that Detective Anton had given me worked their magic as the next thing I knew, Chuck was barking and the door of the cabin opened. Matt sat in the corner of the room as if guarding me and Lucky was snuggled asleep on my stomach. When Detective Anton entered the room, however, Matt left calling Chuck along with him.

Detective Anton crossed the room and perched in front of me concern etched on his forehead and eyes earnest. "Are you okay?" At my nod, he again repeated, "Are you sure you're okay?"

Irritated, I answered back. "I'm just swell. Who wouldn't be?"

That statement must have satisfied him because he got to his feet and said over his shoulder. "Well, I feel better now. You are almost back to your old self."

Entering into the small kitchen, he helped himself to the wine in my fridge, but instead of pouring a glass for just me, he poured two and brought both across the room.

"I thought you didn't drink on duty." Raising brows as he handed a glass to me.

He smiled at me and said. "I'm off duty now." Then he turned but did not sit down at the adjacent rocker, instead he went to the end of the couch, lifted my feet, and sat down, placing my feet in his lap.

My stomach did a somersault. I had trouble being coherent anyway, but this action really tossed in a wrench. Before I could verbalize or make some sense of it all, he began to massage my feet and crooned, similar to the time with Lucky when we didn't know if she would live or die.

"Poor Lily, you've had such a time of it. You are so brave; it has been rough, hasn't it?" He looked at me intently. I was still so dumbfounded by his ministrations that I just uttered. "Well, duh."

At that remark, he hooted and smiled. "You are certainly one of the most passive-aggressive women I have ever met. Such a challenge and a wonder." He chuckled again, and took a sip of his wine.

I could barely sip my wine as between the foot massage and the lingering affects of the earlier medication I could feel myself beginning to drift. I tried to keep awake as the Detective began to talk.

"Dr. Sorenson is the one who killed both Wardell and his wife. Though I'm sure you've figured that out by now. Seems he and Wardell were college chums. Had invested together years ago in California. Wardell was arrested a few years back for fraud and embezzlement. He served a minimal sentence and was released just before he and his wife settled here. What a perfect place, remote, etc., until Sorenson saw and recognized him. The Doctor was still sore because he had lost thousands due to Wardell's misappropriation of funds. Their death's were vengeance, if anything."

I couldn't feel very sorry for the Doctor, reliving his wild eyes and total disregard for mankind.

Continuing on, Detective Anton said. "At first we suspected your boyfriend, an obvious choice, being a newcomer, showing up at the right time, and hard to trace. However he is who he says he is. Thought I may as well pass this on, though, he does have a wife and family back in California. According to his associates, he is off "finding his way."

I was numb already from the events of the day and somehow the news of Peter's personal life did not surprise or hurt as much as I thought it would.

Detective Anton shifted and stood placing my feet gently back on the sofa. "Will you be able to lock up and get yourself to bed?" He queried. I nodded an affirmative and he smiled, bent and tucked my quilt around my feet, ruffled Lucky's fur and left the cabin.

I sat there for a while just thinking about the events of the day, stroking Lucky and how glad I felt to be alive. Finally summoning enough strength, I got up and locked the cabin door then headed for bed.

Wednesday morning arrived with brilliant sun straining through the sheers of my bedroom and directly into my eyes. Rolling onto my side, I attempted continued sleep, but glancing at the bedside clock and seeing that it was after 10 AM, decided I'd better get up.

My back was stiff and sore, most likely from stumbling over the drift the day before and I shuffled like an old woman into the kitchen to check the phone recorder. Two lights were blinking. Poking the play button, I listened to a concerned Gert and just as concerned Dr. Ivers.

I called Gert immediately, not wanting to incur her wrath of earlier when I had been remiss in returning her call. Her concern was genuine and touched my heart. I assured her that I was fine and that I would be over in the morning to enjoy Thanksgiving with her, but that I wasn't in any shape to bring anything homemade for dinner. Her reply was to have me bring myself in one piece.

Dr. Ivers was just as concerned and I was touched. He wanted to know if I needed time off from work to recover. I told him that if Jenny, the vacation replacement, could take my transcription for today, then by Monday I would be ready to go. He was both appreciative and supportive. I hung up the phone feeling much better than I had thought possible.

After cleaning up, I packed a few things in a bag to take to Gert's. That's when I found the two bottles of Chardonnay I had stashed in the pantry after my day with

Peter. Somehow the wine did not harbor the warm memories I originally purchased them for. I reached over to the nearby chair and retrieved my coat. Shrugging into it, I picked up the two bottles of wine and headed out the door.

Matt had evidently brought Chuck home earlier as he slept on the porch and leapt up as I opened the door. He and I walked leisurely, and still a bit stiffly, following the gravel road to the marina and path to the beach.

I had placed a corkscrew in my pocket and sat down upon the sand to open a bottle. The wind blew and my hands were getting chilled. Finally I uncorked the bottle, tilted and poured its contents into the sand. Then, environmentally evil, I raised my arm and threw the bottle deep into the bay as far as I could. Turning, I decided it was too cold to uncork the other bottle, so I tossed it in as well satisfied with the loud splash and disappearance to the bay bottom below. Let the crab, fish or clams enjoy it, for I wouldn't.

Turning, I headed for home, but stopped short. Detective Anton stood on the logs directly behind me. He watched me with no expression on his face, his Columbo style overcoat flapping in the breeze.

"Seems like a waste of good wine." He shouted against the wind.

I climbed up over the logs and walked past him and as I did so, muttered. "No, not such good wine. Just cheap, like the last couple of weeks."

He then said. "Perhaps I should arrest you for littering."

I kept moving, but looked over my shoulder at him and winked. "You'd have to catch me first." Then took off running up the sandy incline with Chuck close at my heels.

Epilogue

The memorial service for Sanford and Vivian the Saturday following Thanksgiving was lovely. Island residents filled the fold-up chairs that lined the small picnic area adjacent to the island clubhouse. Bob and Betty Brummelman, Les and Emma Jean Campbell, the Hansens, and Captain Mike sat in the front few chairs. And, much to my surprise and chagrin, Ralph Waters had flown from Arizona to attend the service as well. He sat in the back row, eyes red and puffy. He was apparently deeply affected by Wardell's demise or sadly going to miss a sparring buddy. We would see, the next time the community board held   another   four-wheeler discussion.

Luckily, the weather proved cooperating, with only a mild breeze to accompany the clear sky. Even the island bald eagles were present. Perched high above on the firs lining the copse behind the clubhouse, they signaled a final farewell. I smiled just then, satisfied that Sanford and Vivian, stuck-up as they had been, would have been pleased with the turnout.

A Pastor from Mukilteo and frequent golf mate of Bob Brummelman's performed the service. I sat wedged between Matt and Lee behind Sanford's brother who had been located by the authorities and who had flown up on Thanksgiving Day from Nevada. He was the mirror image of Sanford, only younger. However, that's where the resemblance ended. For Samuel Wardell was warm and personable, quite the opposite of his brother's remote coolness. Looking at him, I thought about the task of taking care of his brother and sister-in-law's personal affects, as well as their home. According to island gossip, he had already met with a local Realtor and made arrangements for Matt to handle disposal of household furnishings.

I deliberated that the Wardell home would most likely be on the market for a long while, a fact due both to most certainly a high listing price as well as the awkwardness of location. In some ways, I wished I could afford the home. With its opulent luxury and vast space, though what I would do with all of it, I didn't know. No, I reflected, I was much better off in my own rustic abode, with Chuck, Lucky and perhaps occasionally, the ghost of Peter Goutre.

N. R. De Witte

About the Author

N. R. DeWitte was born and raised in the Puget Sound area. She attended college there where she enjoyed many creative writing courses. An avid mystery reader, she was challenged by a colleague to write her own mystery book.

In "It's Murder: On Hat Island" the author revisits the island of her youth and explores the true mysteries of its past. The author is busy writing the second in the series of three books, entitled "It's Mayhem: On Hat Island."

Printed in the United States
21023LVS00001B/37